Angels To Wish By

A Book Of Story-Prayers

by Joseph J. Juknialis

17886

Scriptural texts used in the following stories are from *The New American Bible,* copyright © 1970, by the Confraternity of Christian Doctrine, Washington, DC, and are used by permission: "Perhaps, Perhaps" (I Cor 3:9-11, 16-17; Eph 2:19-22); "givingthanksgiving"; "The Seal" (all except Mt 5:1-12); "The Story"; "One Free Wish"; "The Bag Lady" (Mk 6:30-44); "The Park Bench"; "The Gathering of The Magi" (Lk 2:10b-11a).

The following stories contain excerpts from *The Jerusalem Bible,* copyright © 1966 by Darton, Longman and Todd, Ltd. and Doubleday and Company, Inc., and are used by permission of the publisher: "The Banjo Man"; "Perhaps, Perhaps" (Gen 11:1-9); "Lucy Light"; "The Seal" (Mt 5:1-12); "The Bag Lady" (Jn 6:32, 33, 35, 48-51, 57, 58).

Typography: Sandra Ramirez-Guerrero
Illustrations: Karen Dewey
Mechanical Layout: Karen Dewey

5 4 3

ISBN 0-89390-051-6

Library of Congress Catalog No. 83-061455

Contents

A Christmas Story

Story Prayers

Preface

For us all
there are those fragile moments
when God's gentle presence breaks into our days
    when life truly does become love
    when we become so transparent
        that the holy does show through
when the present is shattered by a future so unimagined
      that joy is its fruit.

Those are the moments we hold as sacred.
They are our angels,
If you will,
for they are the times when God speaks most clearly.
My hope is
that for you
these stories might be such angels,
moments that reveal one more thread of the holy.
With these stories you will also find some wishes
                scriptures
                rituals
                meditations
                all of them wishes.

Some call them prayers,
but prayer
can so often be like time spent
wishing
in the presence of God.
Perhaps, then,
these stories and prayers, together,
may be for you
ANGELS TO WISH BY.

The Gathering of the Magi

In the beginning, Christmas had been created along with all else that God had imagined — with sun and stars and moon, with woman and man and lion and calf, with wolf and lamb and adder and child. Yet for some unknown reason, perhaps ever to remain hidden, Christmas had been lost. Some said it was the chaos of those first unfolding cosmic moments. Others suspected that no one other than God knew the purpose of Christmas, and thus in the beginning no one paid much attention to it. And still others wondered if Christmas had been one more piece of goodness used up in that early struggle for power between the good and bad angels. Whatever the reason, when time came looking for Christmas, Christmas could not be found.

From those first moments, God had created in such a way that all of his love fit together, piece by piece. Everything needed everyone, much as the sea needs the shore. Thus it seemed best to God that he not reorder the confusion himself, but that creation, assured of his presence, search out Christmas in its own way — though perhaps with his nod or a nudge of his love. So it was that God called upon Michael and gave to Michael the task of finding Christmas.

Now Michael was an angel, though some would choose to disagree, for Michael did not look at all like angels are imagined to be. You see, Michael was not tall; he was short — very short — 10 or perhaps 12 inches tall at the most. Nor did Michael wear wings — none at all — and he would be the first to question such a description. Finally, while Michael was not young, no one would ever say he was old. He wondered and smiled like a child; and he had been blessed with ragamuffin hair, a second cousin to the wind. But his eyes twinkled wisdom as someone who has seen much, and the smile with which he spoke lovingly laughed at pain. He was experience returned to innocence. In spite of all those who disagreed, Michael was indeed an angel, delightfully curious and trustingly simple.

As soon as he had been given the task, Michael began to wander the universe, much of which he had not yet seen. He consulted with distant heavens and sought out the oldest and wisest stars. He nudged his way between clouds and waited patiently behind the sun. Though it took much time, having wandered great distances, Michael, nevertheless, refused to fail in his search to find Christmas.

Finally, it was the flighty wind who offered a hint. "It has been reported," suggested the wind, "that of all God's earthly creation, men and women possess the greatest degree of wisdom. Though this has been greatly disputed among many in creation, perhaps you should consult with the creator's people."

"But with which people," wondered Michael aloud. "There are so many. Where should I begin?"

"Perhaps with a king," said the wind in reply. "It would seem," he suggested, "that one who rules people also would possess wisdom."

To Michael, there were any number of kings to ask. Since he knew none of them, he chose one at random — one who seemed not too busy, one reigning on a forgotten hillside, one not bigger in size than a whisper above Michael himself.

Michael thought it best to go in darkness. Then he could slip in quietly while everyone slept. That night, after all in the castle had gone to their rooms, Michael found his way to the chamber of the king.

The king was quite different from what Michael had expected. He wore a crown half his height, a crown which always slipped slightly forward because of its weight. He was short when he stood and short when he sat, always pulling his legs up against his chest and tucking his knees beneath his chin.

And whenever he spoke he would proclaim boldly, "I AM THE KING." But this had been declared so often that no one really heard it anymore. Rather it had become a nervous mannerism of speech without meaning, overlooked by all who talked to the king — all, that is, except Michael, who now spoke with him for the first time.

"Good morning. Who are you? I AM THE KING."

"I am Michael, O king, and I come for your help. I come in search of something lost."

"Of course, of course. What is it you seek? There is nothing I cannot grant. What is it you wish? I AM THE KING." The king stretched tall — as tall as he could — proud that someone would come to him seeking help, since so few of his subjects any longer did.

"I come, O king, in search of Christmas, and wonder if perchance you may have knowledge as to where Christmas may be found."

"In truth, I have not heard of Christmas, but since I am the king, I shall command Christmas to come forth. You see, all in my realm obey my word. All that need be done is for me to speak the command, and Christmas shall come forth. I AM THE KING." By now the king had jumped to his throne and was resting his chin upon his knees, to support his top-heavy crown.

"Excuse me, O king, but I do not think you will find Christmas by commanding her to appear." Michael tried to disagree politely.

With that, the king jumped up and stood on the seat of his royal throne. "And why not, may I ask? I am the king, you know. I AM THE KING."

Michael became confused by the king's many assertions of his royalty. "Most assuredly, you are king, O king. But Christmas cannot be commanded to appear; Christmas is love, and one cannot command love."

"But I am the king — most powerful in the land. Nothing fails to heed my words — not even Christmas. I AM THE KING."

"Christmas, O king, is love," explained Michael, "the love that springs from our hearts and not from our crowns, though both, it would seem, must reign from within and never from without. Love must be given freely, O king, or the Christmas that is love shall die stunted in obligation."

"That cannot be. If that were so, there would be no need for rulers or kings. You are wrong. I shall command Christmas to appear, and you shall see. I AM THE KING."

Michael then understood that he would not find Christmas through the king, so he quietly slipped away, unnoticed by the king. He left the king standing on the cushion of his throne, his crown heavy upon his brow and his arms waving as he cried over and over, "Christmas, I command you to appear. I AM THE KING."

As Michael drifted out and away from the castled home of the king, he noticed a lone workshop light captured in the net of darkness below. Out of curiosity, he slipped down into the darkness only to discover a carpenter shop, its master diligently at work.

The shop looked cluttered to Michael. Half-finished work had been scattered about in corners and on shelves. Shavings and sawdust tinted all with a golden hue, and piles of wood, preserved and unused, waited patiently for their promised worth. At the center of his wooden universe labored the carpenter, a mirrored reflection of his surroundings.

Michael quietly made his way into the workshop by way of the window, thinking he might enter without being noticed by the carpenter. "Yes, yes?" asked the carpenter, never once having looked up. "What is it you wish? I'm quite busy, you know."

"I've come in search of Christmas," explained Michael, wondering if the carpenter knew he was speaking with an angel. "Do you know of Christmas? Have you ever seen Christmas? I would appreciate any help you might be able to give."

"No, I can't say that I've ever seen a Christmas. But if you have a blueprint, I am sure I could build Christmas. Just leave the drawing on the table under the window and come back in a week," continued the carpenter, never glancing up to acknowledge a world beyond his workbench. "I am a master carpenter, you know. I have built the finest of whatever has been needed — homes for the old, tables to serve those we love, and carriages to bring them to our tables. Indeed, I shall build Christmas for you."

"Excuse me, master carpenter," said Michael, "but I do not think you will be able to build Christmas with the skills of your trade."

Such disagreement so startled the carpenter that he almost lifted his head to look at who it was who dared to challenge his skills. But in that same moment his eye caught sight of a flaw in the wood. Immediately he forgot the voice with which he spoke, and his attention fully returned once more to his work. In a moment he remembered his conversation, but only verbally did he return to it. "Why, may I ask, do you think I shall be unable to build Christmas? I am a master carpenter, you know."

"Most assuredly, you are a master, O carpenter. Yet Christmas cannot be built, for Christmas is light. It cannot be shaped by your tools." Michael found himself wishing the carpenter would cast a glance his way to offer at least a sliver of his own light in recognition of his guest. But none came.

"Nonsense. I am a carpenter, master of all in the land. There is nothing I am unable to build — even Christmas."

"Christmas, O carpenter, is light," repeated Michael. "True, one does live in light, but the light that is Christmas is much grander than a castle and can never be built. Yes, one is born wrapped in a cradle of light, and one dies journeying in a carriage into light, but such cradles and such carriages can never be built with hands. You see, Christmas is the light that guards us from fear and reveals the God who loves."

Just then the carpenter discovered another flaw in the wood, and again focused his attention on his work. "Show me the plans," he mumbled. "Show me the plans."

Michael realized then that he had not been heard, indeed, never even seen. As he faded through the window by which he had arrived, he wondered if the carpenter would remember their conversation.

As Michael took leave of the carpenter's workshop, he noticed that dawn had not yet begun to unfold, though the morning star had already been hung as a nightlight for the sun. In the early morning darkness, the shopkeepers and merchants were already preparing for the coming day's business. With the hope that perhaps one of them might know of Christmas, Michael made his way down the back alleys in search of someone who seemed friendly enough to help. He stopped at the door of a merchant known for the fine goods with which he traded. The merchant's door was open to welcome the morning freshness, and Michael made his way into the shop.

Once inside he began to look for the owner. Strange, thought Michael, that the door would be open with no one inside. Then he heard a jingling — not constant, not regular, but certainly present. Again and again he heard the jingling, always moving, always interrupted, first from behind one shelf of expensive wares, then from behind another. Finally the source of the jingling was revealed. It was the merchant.

Imposing and self-assured, arrayed in the finest of his own goods, the merchant stood before Michael. His hair was a narrow band of yellowing white, the ends of which were tucked over each ear. He had grown a full white beard that blanketed his chin and came to rest on a belly as well stocked as the shop in which he worked.

Over and about his clothing the merchant wore coins — coins in a chain over his shoulders, coins sewn to the hem of his garment and the cuffs of his sleeves, coins linked as a belt about his well-fed belly, and coins loose in his pockets for bartering

and trading. When he smiled, he also jingled, for he smiled with his entire body. Thus there was an almost constant jingling of coins whenever he was in his shop, for there he was in constant delight over the wealth he would attain from the sale of his goods.

"May I be of help?" inquired the merchant as he smiled and jingled.

"Oh, yes," answered Michael. "I hope so. I've come in search of Christmas which has been lost and now is in need of being found. Can you help?"

At once the merchant perceived the opportunity to enter a bargain and increase his wealth, and as he did so, he smiled broadly. Immediately the sound of jingling coins increased. "Of course. I'd be most delighted to help. Indeed, you've come to the right place."

"Then you know of Christmas? You know where Christmas can be found?" asked Michael.

"Well, no, not yet at least. But I shall go forth and buy Christmas. Return this evening, and I will have purchased what you have lost. My name is known throughout the land as the shrewdest of all traders and the cleverest of all in striking a bargain. No, there is nothing I am unable to purchase, nothing I am unable to attain, though I must caution you, the price may be high. But if you are willing to pay the cost, I assure you I will have Christmas for you no later than this eve."

Again Michael found himself disagreeing. "Oh, I fear, fine merchant, that perhaps your efforts shall find little success, for I do not believe you will be able to locate the product you seek."

"Not so! Not so!" The jingling now grew quieter as the merchant, fearful of losing a sale, protested. "Not so! For I am a merchant. Never — I say, never — have I failed to complete an order once placed."

"That may be so," insisted Michael, "but Christmas, you see, is peace. That is why Christmas cannot be purchased — not by you or by anyone. Peace can be had only by those willing to offer forgiveness, and forgiveness must be given freely. When it is paid for or given under a condition, what could have been

14

forgiveness instead becomes revenge and hurt. Then there is no peace. No, fine merchant, clever though you may be, no fortune shall you ever offer or receive in exchange for Christmas."

"Then it must be that Christmas does not exist," declared the merchant, "for whatever is not able to be purchased, in truth, is not — not now, or ever."

In that moment the jingling surrendered to the silence while the merchant and Michael stood by. Michael then took leave of the merchant, and the silence that remained quietly revealed the absence of peace.

No sooner had Michael left the merchant's shop and made his way out of the alley and into the street, than he noticed a glimmer of light bounce out of a storefront window and into the darkness. The glimmer had nearly been missed, almost lost in the dawned confusion that surrounds the exchange between nighttime and day. A sign hung above the window revealing the shop of a seamstress, and the window itself revealed her work — magnificent garments sewn with perfection and adorned with fashion and good taste.

Michael wondered if the glimmer was light once discarded by some star ages past, a star that would have known of Christmas. So he slipped into the shop — though only for a moment — lest the nighttime darkness depart without him, thereby revealing his comings and goings.

The inside of the shop reflected the personality of the seamstress as much as did the garments she sewed. Both were designed with the belief that perfection brought beauty and fanciful fashion provided joy. The seamstress indeed saw no splendor in the simple. Even her own appearance was that of one for whom the garments were sewn, of one who lived in elegance. Always she was arrayed in perfection. Her graying hair she wore painstakingly styled, never a hair out of place. For the last 30 years, her hands had been manicured weekly. In the end, her desire for delicate detail and her fondness for fashion designed her into someone whose happiness was as fragile as the lace she sewed.

All this Michael quickly perceived and sensed it futile even to ask. Yet out of politeness he posed the question he had borne from stranger to stranger. Had she, the seamstress, happened upon Christmas?

"Christmas?" she puzzled.

"Yes. Do you know of Christmas?"

"Well, I know there is nothing I cannot design and sew," replied the seamstress. "If it is Christmas you wish, I shall create for you a most beautiful garment fashioned out of cloth of gold and sewn with thread spun from silver. Should you wish, I could adorn Christmas with jewels, for I have diamonds brighter than a guiding star and rubies more breathtaking than angels arrayed in song. Tell me what you wish and I shall fashion you a Christmas as magnificent as you have ever dreamed."

"I fear you have misunderstood," Michael told her gently. "I come, madam seamstress, in search of Christmas. But you propose to fashion me a garment of precious metal and glittering jewels."

"Of course, of course. It is so; it is so. Tell me what you wish, and I shall begin to sew at once."

"Madame seamstress, may I explain? I fear you too have misunderstood, as did the king and the carpenter and the merchant. Christmas, you see, is joy. Yet joy is found deep within, never put on as easily as one's garment or one's coat. Joy can never be designed as a copy of what one imagines. If ever joy were a garment, it would be sewn of one's spirit, magnificent in its simplicity and of worth beyond measure. Christmas is joy, madam seamstress, a garment, true, but woven within one's heart, whole, without need of being sewn."

"Lace, you wish?" she asked. "Is that not so? Very well, lace, for you speak well. Yes, Christmas is joy and lace brings joy."

"No! No! You do not understand," insisted Michael.

"Then silk. You wish joy, I will use silk." The seamstress began to rummage through her chests of threads and garment frills, mumbling to herself something about lace and silk, about Christmas and joy. Without her realizing it, her fondness for fashion had turned to fetish. She never even noticed Michael making his way out of her store. She only continued to mumble over the fabrics of fine fashion — a futile search in the midst of that which destroyed the very thing she sought.

Out on the street once more, Michael realized that the night was quickly coming to a close. Already the day had been proclaimed victor, though enough nighttime still clung to the edges of the sky. While Michael wished to make one more visit, enough time did not remain. But the night then offered to linger a bit longer that morning, in order that Michael might make his one last visit. It was to a scholar that Michael yet wished to pose the question.

He found the scholar alone at the edge of the realm, mentally chained to the book-lined walls of his self-imposed prison. Here he lived a reality bound in volumes rather than people and numbered by pages rather than by years. He delighted in other people's insights, considered other people's thoughts, burned with other people's passions, and loved by ink on a page rather than by the touch of a hand or the word of one close. For most, reality was destroyed when love was lost; for the scholar the destruction of his books would have erased the meaning of life.

Thus the scholar was not much confused when asked by Michael if he had known Christmas. If it had been written, he would have known Christmas.

"You look for Christmas?" inquired the scholar. "Allow me a day's time and I shall know her well. In my library I have the finest books in the realm. I shall study Christmas and understand her thoroughly. With research I shall come to know her. I shall reflect and consider as well as ponder and muse. With skill I shall reason and deliberate. My mind shall speculate and cogitate, and so meditate and appreciate. Than I shall be able to define for you that which you seek — Christmas, no less."

"Wise scholar, might I suggest that Christmas cannot be learned, for Christmas is in one's spirit. You see, Christmas is hope, and as such is not found in a book."

"Nonsense! Nonsense!" muttered the scholar as he peered over his glasses, paging through a huge volume marked only by a large, red, Roman numeral. "Hmm," he muttered again, leafing back and forth from one chapter to the next, occasionally checking with another volume. Suddenly, he said, "I have it! I have it! Hush now and I shall define Christmas."

> Christmas is that sequential environment both seasonal and temporal, surrounding the natal event in time of the divine inclination to manifest itself in human history. While it is theologically rooted in ecclesial faith, it has the ability to accrue to itself profound social and psychological meaning thereby achieving almost universal approbation.

Michael feared the scholar did not understand. "If I may, wise scholar, might I suggest once more that Christmas is hope. It is rooted, not in volumes of recorded human thought, but in the human spirit which no recorded account can ever fully convey. Christmas is the hope in a God who loves us and whose love can never be contained in a book or a definition or a concept. Christmas is the sure hope that God lives, playing hide-and-go-seek with human hearts who trust in the promise that he can and will be found."

"Yes, yes. But where do you find this?" asked the scholar. "What book holds this knowledge? Are you sure of what you say? I must confess I have not read of it before."

"To read of the hope that is Christmas, one must only read the human heart. It cannot be found in any book," said Michael quietly.

"No book, you say? No book! Then Christmas cannot be known. In all of human wisdom, I tell you, you search in vain. Indeed, Christmas cannot be known."

With that the scholar became satisfied that the question had been resolved. He turned back to his books and the dusty candlelight that now served as a crutch to the dying darkness. Michael left sadly then, and returned to the edge of the sky where the night waited patiently. Together they silently disappeared, to the notice of no one. Christmas had still not been found.

That new day, fragile in its beginning, almost died in birth, so weak was it with promise. Yet a strange thread of events was to weave it a garment of strength and warmth.

No sooner had the night and Michael dissolved into the horizon, than the king began to make his way through the village streets. To all the villagers it was obvious he had not slept the entire night, and his crown rode heavy on his brow. He came trudging down the street, shouting, "Christmas, I command you to come forth. I AM THE KING." By midday he no longer shouted commands, and he no longer insisted, "I AM THE KING." Instead he went from door to door seeking ordinary wisdom on the whereabouts of Christmas. There were some in the village who reported that they had seen the king in later afternoon without his crown — a most unusual report to be sure.

At about the same time the king was seen coming into the village, the carpenter was seen leaving, climbing up into the wooded hillsides above the village. There, he later told the villagers, he spent the day in search of light, for he had been told by some unknown visitor the night before that Christmas was light. What it was he sought, he was not sure, but he sensed he would recognize it when he came upon it.

The merchant and the seamstress both found themselves wrapped in days not much different from either the king's or the carpenter's. While the merchant journeyed from one nearby village to the next, in hope of coming upon a shop stored with enough Christmas to sell, the seamstress designed and sewed garment after garment, all the while clinging to fantasies of fine fashion. By day's end, the merchant returned home silently unsuccessful, having neither smiled nor jingled. The seamstress, on the other hand, had been reduced to poverty, for as each fantasied creation failed to produce the Christmas that is joy, she would destroy it and discard it in frustration and disappointment.

The scholar had decided that since none of his books contained knowledge of Christmas, somewhere there must be a book of which he had not heard. Thus he spent his day knocking at each door in the village, seeking an imagined book of imagined wisdom so that he might imagine himself a scholar. As darkness bore the end of day, he was no wiser.

Thankful for the darkness that allowed him to hide his failure, the scholar now directed his steps back through the village to the security of his book stacks. He clutched at the shadows as he came to the center of the village, grateful to the nighttime chill that kept the villagers inside. Suddenly, from his darkened sanctuary, he heard the weeping of a slumped shadow. Torn between continuing and stopping, he moved toward whoever it was who sat there in the sadness. The scholar realized, then, it was the king, vulnerable and weak, who wept. The king, fearful of being laughed at, looked up. But instead of humiliation he saw understanding eyes. What the volumes of wisdom had not taught the scholar, that day's visits to the people of the village had — that weakness and fear and a need to be loved were written in the hearts of all people, rulers and villagers alike.

Unlocked by the kindness he saw, the king trusted the scholar with the events of that day and of the night before. In the end, he told of how he had failed as king — failed in his efforts to find Christmas. When he finished, the scholar simply shook his head in disagreement. "One failure," the scholar explained, "does not turn life into failure. Instead, it is the one avenue to wisdom, for by one's own weakness one is able to overlook the weakness in others and see the real goodness that is in the heart of all who

21

are human." Indeed, the scholar surprised himself at the gentleness of his own advice.

The scholar went on to tell the king, then, that when he saw him so saddened, he realized how deeply human even a king could be, how fragile even a royal person is. Seeing the king so simple and honest, explained the scholar, caused his own heart to go out to him. The scholar told the king, then, how he did care for him, how he seemed so much in pain. Finally, after all else had been said, the scholar told the king that he had come to love him — to love him for no other reason but that he was so human and shared in the same struggles as everyone else.

When the king heard such kindness and learned that he was even loved, the light in his eyes shone brighter with tears of happiness that sparkled in the nighttime cold. He was about to tell the scholar how much his kindness meant when the two were joined by the merchant, who happened upon them quite by accident. He was making his way back to his shop from the last village to which he had gone in the hope of purchasing Christmas.

The moment was awkward, for the merchant was guilty of cheating on his yearly taxes, and the fact was well known to all, including the king. He was about to back away into the dark cold of the night without saying a word when the king stepped forward and held him by the shoulder. Weakened by guilt, the merchant grew fearful, sure that the king was about arrest him for not paying his full taxes. Instead, the king smiled and told the merchant what had just taken place between himself and the scholar, and how he had come to know he was loved. Not sure why he was made privy to such knowledge, the merchant grew confused, yet he was too afraid to take leave. Finally, the king explained that just as he had been gifted with the knowledge of being loved, so he wished to gift the merchant and offer him pardon and forgiveness for not paying his taxes. The debt was to be cancelled, freely and without punishment, never to be alluded to again.

The merchant was awestruck. Never in his wildest dreams had he expected such kindness — to be forgiven for his greed by the one he had harmed. In that moment, he was overcome by a peace that welled up from deep within. Never again would he be the same. A new light had been born. He began to smile. His entire body smiled. Yet his coins did not jingle. The merchant had been made new.

There in the center of the village stood the king and the scholar and the merchant, bound in silence more still than the breath of their spirits, bound in light more powerful than the night that held them.

The merchant was about to voice his appreciation when the attention of all three was drawn to a corner of the darkness that had been creased by someone's movement. He called out to whoever it was who had all but torn the moment of light. It was the seamstress who stepped forth, fearful and disheveled.

When asked what she had been doing there, she apologized with tears and trembling. As it turned out, she had realized that in her frustration to design and sew Christmas, she also had destroyed and discarded all of her fashionable fabric of gold and silver-drawn thread, all of the lace and silk that had been designed to bring joy. By day's end, her poverty was all that remained. She had been made sadly weak, and her fear was made worse by being forced to confess her failure to her rival, the merchant.

She fully expected to be ridiculed and laughed at. Instead, the merchant, who had been so transformed by the king's forgiveness and the peace it brought, offered her all the coins he carried — those about his shoulders and his waist, those sewn to the hems of his garments, all those carried in his pockets for barter. He had set out to purchase Christmas; instead he gave away the one power he treasured, and he did it with such gentleness and kindness that the seamstress never felt bound in obligation or servitude.

In that moment of generosity, the seamstress was robed in a joyful beauty she had never been able to fashion. Someone cared about her, and in the weakness of her poverty she was filled with a joyful light she could not explain. Never had such joy been sewn with her hands. Alone, she had been helpless to bring it about. Never again, she insisted, would she spend her days fashioning fantasies of what had been such fragile beauty.

The scholar, who until now had simply watched the exchange between king and merchant and between merchant and seamstress, suddenly realized how each had come in weakness and how the weakness had become the means to new life. The king, whom the scholar had come upon in failure, found himself loved and offered peace. The merchant had come shrouded in grief and, having been raised to the new life of peace, grew generous and blessed the seamstress with joy. The seamstress arrived in poverty and, having been gifted with joy, came to possess a simple beauty never again to be lost. In that moment the scholar saw that people could change, that it was possible for people to become more than what they had been. The future, he realized, held more promise than the past. He now knew that with human love and peace and joy it was possible to write of a day so new that it was not yet even dreamed of, much less written about, by any author of old. He who had come seeking a knowledge of Christmas had discovered instead a newborn hope written in the human heart. With that hope, the darkness seemed less powerful, the night less fearful, the cold less chilling. The light of hope had been born in the weakness of knowledge unknown.

The tale of the carpenter's day yet remains to be shared. As was told earlier, he had left in the morning dawn and journeyed up into the wooded hillsides above the village in search of light so that he might build Christmas. He wandered the loggers' roads, and he traced the hikers' paths. His eyes searched the hollowed caves of the hillsides as well as the caverned clouds of the sky. Nowhere was he able to find the light of which Christmas is made.

As darkness fell, the carpenter realized he had wandered far into a forest that held nothing familiar. Wrapped in blinding darkness, his spirit confessed the helplessness he felt. Forced to surrender to the night, he grew cold and fearful. Powerless to find his way and powerless to build Christmas, he sat down and leaned back against a rock. In that moment of surrender, he

looked into the distance and saw a faint glimmer of light. He blinked once, then twice to make sure. It was indeed a thin shadow of light, just enough to be his guide.

The carpenter followed the light he saw. Slowly, as he made his way toward it, it grew brighter and brighter. Soon it was brilliant enough so he could recognize a path he had trod earlier in the day. Closer and closer he came to the village and to his home. His spirit breathed new life.

Finally, he arrived at the center of the village, only to find the king and the scholar, the merchant and the seamstress. The four sat there in the gentle darkness. It seemed no brighter there than anywhere else in the village, yet unmistakably they were the source of the light that had led him home.

He told them, then, of how he had been helplessly lost and graciously found, and all of the others, in turn, told how they too had been newly gifted at the very moment when they realized their own helplessness. The king had found love and the merchant peace. The seamstress had been gifted with joy and the scholar with hope. Together their blessings had been light, sufficient for the carpenter to be led home.

There in the center of the village, those who had once been visited by Michael in search of Christmas sat in prayerful silence. Their spirits had grown wise and their hearts one. Christmas had been found. Though Michael had returned to witness the discovery, no one there was aware of his presence as he sat in the village shadows. He smiled quietly, content that his task had been completed, and then silently took his leave. Yes, Christmas had been found, and though few noticed, high in the sky a lone star grew brighter and brighter as it came to rest above that holy moment. In that silence an angel spoke:

I come to proclaim good news to you — tidings
of great joy to be shared by the whole people.
This day in David's city a savior has been
born to you.

(*Luke* 2:10-11)

One Free Wish

To this day my mother will tell you that as I grew up, I had an imaginary friend named Josh. Contrary to all she says, however, he was real. There was a time when I tried to explain how I met him and what he looked like, yet at this time it makes little difference if anyone else believes in him. I knew him, and in many ways my life is different because of him.

There is in northeastern Wisconsin a peninsula of land which juts out into Lake Michigan from the body of the state like a thumb from one's hand. It is known as Door County. In the early years of my childhood our family would often spend weekends and occasionally an entire week's vacation in Door county. My brother was still too young to accompany me on my jaunts into the wilds of Door County, so I often journeyed alone into what was as yet to me unknown and uncharted territory. I marked the beaches with castles of sand, mapped in my mind the rocky coastland, and memorized the inland paths that connected the two. By the time I was six, there was no doubt in my mind that I knew the ways of Door County.

It was on one such adventure in Door County that Josh found me. Later I came to realize that Josh always found me. It was never I who found him, even though there were many times when I went out to look for him. It was always he who slipped up while I was building sandy turrets as sentinels against the sea. It was always he who joined my path, fifty steps behind, as I explored the rocky coast.

Josh was very much like Door County, and to have known him was to have known that special place. To me he was like a grandpa, though I could not say for sure that he was that old. In those days of my life, anyone who wore a beard was a grandpa. He wore an old, brown, tweed sportcoat with sleeves so frayed that the loose threads often would tickle my face when he playfully brushed my tousled hair. The pockets on the sportcoat were always bulgy and stretched, even when they were empty, for in the fall Josh always came with the pockets filled with apples. Indeed, he even smelled sweet like Door County apples.

There were times, too, when Josh would invite me to his cabin, a tiny place with two rooms — one for sleeping and one for eating and visiting. In front there lived an old, wooden, picket fence, which looked much like Josh, with pickets that were once new and freshly white, and now dusty grey from the wind that had brushed by for years long past. In summer, there was always a bowl of Door County cherries sitting on Josh's kitchen table. Always he would let me eat as many cherries as I wished — something my mother would never allow. And when I finished the bowl, Josh would fill it up again. Like Door County, Josh's bowl held more than enough cherries to satisfy.

In early summer, Josh would smell like the lake — no, not fishy like the lake in late summer, but rather fresh and crisp like the lake being born. Josh's hands were often covered with artist oils. Indeed, the backs of his hands looked like the palettes of one who committed to canvass the dreams of the earth. In the winter months, Josh's beard would be covered with sawdust and shavings, for his artistic spirit shaped wood as well as canvas. As I said before, to have known Josh was to have known Door County. They were, it seemed, one and the same.

During those first days when I had met Josh I told my mother about my new friend. At first she was not overly concerned, it seemed to me, but as I spoke of him more frequently, and as her inquiries among Door county residents failed to confirm my stories, she grew a bit suspicious of Josh's existence. The first time I told her of my visit to his cabin, she seemed a bit more concerned and asked if I might show her where Josh lived. I tried to find his home, but Josh and his cabin always seemed to find me, rather than the other way around. In the end, my mother was firmly convinced that Josh was indeed an imaginary friend.

During the summer that I turned seven, our family spent an entire week in Door County. Early in the week, Josh found me along the beach. We exchanged stories about all that had taken place since we had last seen each other. Then Josh invited me to his cabin, explaining he had something special there for me, something he had been saving for a long time. He wanted me to have it because, he said, he thought I was special.

We laughed and talked as we walked together to Josh's cabin. And though the paths seemed familiar, somehow I never did remember to find my own way there. When we arrived, Josh took me to his back yard, where we picked ripe red cherries from his trees. When we had enough, Josh sat down on an old wooden crate beneath a large, shady, apple tree, and invited me to come sit on his lap. I sensed that this was the moment Josh was going to give me his special gift, so, without being told, I squeezed my eyes tight and stretched out both hands, side-by-side. Josh laughed out loud at my excitement, and at my anticipation of what was about to take place. I knew his laugh came from his love and not from his ridicule. "No, no, Joey," he smiled. "You don't have to close your eyes." Josh held a closed hand facing downward out over mine. Slowly he opened his hand and pulled it back. Quickly I blinked, twice, perhaps three times, for I could see nothing. "There's nothing there," I said. "My hand is empty." "No, no," said Josh, "only you must see it with your spirit and not with your eyes." I was not sure I understood.

Karen Dewey

"What you hold," said Josh, "is a wish — one free wish. Hold it gently, Joey," he cautioned, "for it is the only one you shall ever own. With it you can wish once for whatever you think you might want. But before you make your wish, think carefully lest you waste it on something foolish. When you make your wish, Joey, I will write it upon your heart, and there it shall be for all of your days."

Immediately the eyes of my spirit began to seel all sorts of possibilities, all sorts of things I had always wanted in my wildest daydreams. Quickly Josh read the rhythm in my dancing eyes, and before I was able to speak my wish, he warned, "Think twice, Joey. If it is money you want, know that there is much worth more than such wealth." I was a bit surprised that Josh could so readily ream my mind. "Consider for a moment, Joey," he went on, "that indeed the health of your body is worth much more than all else that you might own. But," he added, "before you choose, go home and think about your wish. Tomorrow will be soon enoght to decide. There is no rush, no hurry."

Slowly I placed my wish into the pocket of my pants. Though Josh and I spoke of other things as we walked back to the beach, the wish that rested gently in my pocket could not be forgotten.

That night, after our family had finished supper and while my mother packed away the dishes, I lingered in the kitchen, trying to find a way to ask her what she might choose were she given one free wish. I only knew that I had to make something terribly important sound unimportant in the asking, lest I reveal my secret in my question. "Joey," she finally asked, "you're so under foot tonight. What's the matter with you? Are you worried about something?"

"No, not really," I said, trying to act casual. "I was just wondering. If you had one free wish for anything at all you wanted, what would you choose?"

"Oh, I don't know," she sighed. "I suppose I'd ask for good health. Without good health, nothing else is worth much at all. Why do you ask?"

"Oh, I don't know. I was just wondering, I guess." Inside I kept telling myself to remain calm even though my spirit wanted to shout in celebration. Josh was right. My mom was right. They both agreed, and since I loved them both, that had to be the right answer. I could hardly wait till morning when I would see Josh and tell him I was ready to make my wish.

I woke early, much like when I would wake to see if Santa Claus had come on Christmas morning. No one else in my family had gotten up yet, and so, alone, I slipped away from the cottage and made my way to the shore, hoping that Josh would not be long in finding me. I had been at the shore barely five minutes when Josh appeared high above me on a cliff. He called out and waved his arm as I ran up to tell him my decision.

"Josh, Josh, I know what I'm going to wish for. You were right. Money isn't the best thing. You want to know my wish? You want to know?"

"Oh, Joey," smiled Josh. "Don't tell me yet, for once it's spoken, the wish is made, only to be written on your heart to last all your days. Are you sure of your wish, Joey? Are you sure?"

"Yes, yes. I really know, Josh. I really do."

"Well, before you tell me, let me just say this. It may be that you decided to choose good health for all your days, but consider this before you choose. Love is an even greater gift than health. You see, when one is loved and also offers love, then the deepest hurts and pains are often healed as well. Love, Joey, is a most powerful force."

He must have seen the disappointment in my eyes, then, for he stooped down, put his arms around me and hugged me. He told me not to worry, that I would make the right choice in the end. He was sure, he said, and told me he would be back the following day. Then, he said, having thought about it one more day, I could tell him what it was I had decided to wish for. Josh smiled, waved once more, and slowly walked home. On any other day I would surely have chased along, but this day I stayed near the shore hoping that the waves would wash smooth the rugged confusion of my mind.

How does a boy choose wisely when he is given one free wish? I spent the day wrapped in such wondering. In the end, I decided that Josh would know more than I — right or wrong. It would be his suggestion I would take, whatever it would be. The following morning I again made my way to the beach, though not quite as early and with not quite the excitement of the day before.

Before noon, Josh found me once again. He noted quickly that my enthusiasm was not quite what it had been the day before. "Did you decide, Joey?" he asked.

"Uh huh," I shook my head in agreement. "But I'm scared, Josh, I really am. What if I make the wrong decision? What if I don't choose the right thing? Then what? Well, anyway, Josh, you're so smart and there's so much that you know, I decided that I'd choose whatever you thought best. Since you think love is best, I've decided to make my wish and choose..."

"No, no, not yet, Joey. There is one thing more you must consider. Even greater than love is wisdom, for if one is wise there is much one can understand — the why's of wealth and also its lack, of health and illness as well. Why, with wisdom, Joey, one also comes to know how best to love deeply and also the why's of the suffering that always journeys with love. Before you choose, Joey, consider wisdom and all its blessings."

I thought for a moment and was about to make wisdom my wish, since it seemed that Josh thought it best. Instead, Josh interrupted my thoughts once more. "No, Joey, don't make your wish just yet. Think about it one more day. Tomorrow for sure we shall make your wish and decide together what it is you might choose. Tomorrow I shall at last write it upon your heart, there to remain all your days."

I remember thinking that it was all beginning to seem a bit silly, this continual choosing and waiting. Yet, since I had decided to follow Josh's lead, I would go along with what he said. For the remainder of the day and during that evening, I again began to grow excited, for Josh had promised that the next day would be the day of choosing.

The sunlight of the following morning found my father gently nudging me awake. "It's time to get up, Joey. Our vacation's almost over. We have to be heading home soon," he said.

"No, no," I pleaded. "Not yet. I have to see Josh one more time. I have to make my wish. We can't leave yet."

My father wasn't sure what I was talking about and wondered about the wish, I could tell, but he only said to hurry. There wasn't much time before we would leave. I tried to find Josh that morning but as always he could not be found. Nor did Josh find me. When it came time to leave, I carried in my pocket one, unused, free wish. True, I could make the wish on my own, but somehow it seemed that it should be made when Josh was there. He was, after all, the one who had given the gift. And besides, he had promised that he would write it upon my heart. I needed to have Josh there when I made my wish.

All of this took place when I was seven years old. For all sorts of reasons I never returned to Door County — not until I was 27. During the 20 years that passed, I never used my one free wish, though I continued to carry it with me wherever I went. In the beginning, I think I carried it in hopes of a chance meeting with Josh. But as I grew older, I found myself wondering about it and for what it would best be used. There were any number of times when I was about to make that one free wish, yet I always found myself hesitating long enough to remember how Josh always suggested something greater or wiser.

Though I have returned to Door County many times since, never once have I found Josh, never once has Josh found me, never once has the wish been made. Yet the wish's greatest gift has been the freedom to dream, to imagine what could be, to believe that somewhere there is someone who will write it upon my heart there to remain all my days.

A reading from the book of the prophet Jeremiah

The days are coming, says the Lord, when I will make a new covenant with the house of Israel and the house of Judah. It will not be like the covenant I made with their fathers the day I took them by the hand to lead them forth from the land of Egypt; for they broke my covenant, and I had to show myself their master, says the Lord. But this is the covenant which I will make with the house of Israel after those days, says the Lord. I will place my law within them, and write it upon their hearts; I will be their God, and they shall be my people. No longer will they have need to teach their friends and kinsmen how to know the Lord. All, from least to greatest, shall know me, says the Lord, for I will forgive their evil doing and remember their sin no more. (Jer 31:31-34)

Good and Holy, Lasting and True
a Homily for Marriage

There are those who would say that the occurrence first took place among the native Americans of our land. Others would say that they learned of it from those settlers who passed through those Indian tribes. And yet others will tell you it is a tale yet to take place, but one also born once in the dreams of lovers. Where this tale comes from, or if it ever took place, makes little difference. What is important is that it be told, and that it be told now, for it is a story of love as we celebrate that gift today.

One day a young man and a young woman met. They grew to love one another deeply and longed to spend all of their days with one another. Thus the two came to the elder of the village and asked him if they could be joined in marriage. The elder looked at them and simply smiled. He would agree, he explained, if they would answer his one question. If they knew the answer, he said, they would be ready for marriage. They agreed, and asked what the question might be. It is this, he said. Tell me, if you can, what it is that makes a marriage good and holy, lasting and true. The young man and the young woman turned to one another and saw in each other's eyes that neither knew. They confessed their ignorance to the elder, but he simply reminded them of the conditions to which they both had agreed. When they learned the answer, he continued to explain, he would witness their love and proclaim them one in marriage.

The young man and the young woman left the elder's presence and wandered through the land, wondering how they might come to know what it is that makes a marriage good and holy, lasting and true. It was the young man who thought that perhaps the moon might know, for it was in the light of the moon that they first came to discover their love for one another. Thus the two journeyed to the moon to discover what it is that makes a marriage good and holy, lasting and true.

When they came upon the moon washing in beauty and silent wonder, the two posed their question. Would the moon, they wondered aloud, know the answer they both sought? But alas, the moon did not know. But how could that be, they questioned further, for it was in her light that they had fallen in love

many seasons earlier. That may have been, explained the moon, but she knew only of love and not marriage. She could not explain what it is that makes a marriage good and holy, lasting and true.

The young man and the young woman then continued to wander among creation, still wondering who might reveal to them the wisdom they sought. It was the young woman who suggested that perhaps the lake would know, for both she and the young man had often peered into the lake's depths to see themselves reflected off of her calm, silent surface. So they journeyed to the lake and asked if she might know what it is that makes a marriage holy and good, lasting and true. The lake only rippled and said that she did not know. But how could that be, they both wondered, for so often they had seen their own goodness and beauty reflected in her waters. Could she not then know the knowledge they sought? If, when you peered into my depths you saw goodness and beauty, that may be, explained the lake, but that is only because when you both came you already shared that goodness and beauty. You see, I can reflect only what is already present; what it is that makes it so I do not know. So it was that the young man and the young woman slowly walked away from the lake, still unable to enter into the marriage they sought.

In the days that followed the young man and the young woman journeyed to many in God's creation. They sought out the wind and the stars, the birds and the clouds, the flowers and the snowflakes. Always they asked what it is that makes a marriage holy and good, lasting and true. And always they left no wiser than when they had asked.

Finally the two returned to the elder in the village. They explained how they had traveled throughout all of creation without finding anyone who could tell them the answer to the elder's question. Having heard of their quest and the journey they'd traveled, the elder smiled at the two so much in love, much as he had first smiled long ago before they began their journey. He then took the two by their hands and led them to the center of the village. There, all in the village gathered about the young man and the young woman in one unbroken circle of love. One by one, they came forth to tell the young man and the young woman what it is that makes a marriage holy and good, lasting and true.

At this point in the story, members of the congregation come forward with gifts for the bride and the groom. Each makes his or her statement in words similar to those that follow, offers his or her gift to the bride and groom, and then returns to his or her place. Those who come may be parents, wedding attendants, or individuals from the congregation who are particularly close to the bride and groom.

Flower: John and Jenny, as the flower is gentle, so you must be gentle with one another — gentle, so that forgiveness will not be difficult. For you must forgive one another as did Jesus, if your marriage is to be holy and good, lasting and true.

Cross: John and Jenny, you must live your life with faith. It must be your faith that gives meaning to all you do. Not power. Not wealth. Not love of self. You must live your life in faith, as did Jesus, if your marriage is to be good and holy, lasting and true.

Rings: John and Jenny, your love must be patient, giving sufficient time to one another for growth. The time of your love must be forever, as was the love of Jesus, if your marriage is to be holy and good, lasting and true.

Wine: John and Jenny, wine brings joy to those who gather. So must you be a source of joy for one another, as was Jesus, if your marriage is to be holy and good, lasting and true.

Bread: John and Jenny, bread sustains, in trials and in difficulties. So you must be bread for one another, as was Jesus, if your marriage is to be holy and good, lasting and true.

After all those who had gathered had made their gift, after all had returned to their places in that one unbroken circle of love, the entire community stood. With the young man and the young woman seated in their midst, they all extended their arms over the heads of that young man and that young woman. With hands extended, those who had gathered bowed their heads and silently prayed that the young man and young woman might be bound by their love for all of their days.

As the above paragraph is being told, the celebrant gestures at the appropriate times for the community to stand, to extend their arms in the traditional blessing gesture, to bow their heads, and to pray in silence. All this is done without verbal directions, only with accompanying gestures.

After those who had gathered had prayed, they were all once more seated. Then the young man and young woman, having learned what it is that makes a marriage holy and good, lasting and true, were brought forward to the center of that community. There, in the midst of all who had gathered, they professed their undying love for one another.

At this point the bride and groom come forward before the assembled community and vow their love for one another.

The Park Bench

A reading from the holy Gospel according to John.

Jesus looked up to heaven and prayed:
"Holy Father,
I do not pray for my disciples alone.
I pray also for those who will believe in me through their word,
that all may be one
as you, Father, are in me, and I in you;
I pray that they may be one in us,
that the world may believe that you sent me.
I have given them the glory you gave me
that they may be one, as we are one —
I living in them, you living in me —
that their unity may be complete.
So shall the world know that you sent me,
and that you loved them as you loved me."
(Jn 17:20-23)

-or-

A reading from the holy Gospel according to John.

Jesus said to his disciples:
"As the Father has loved me,
so I have loved you.
Live on in my love.
You will live in my love
if you keep my commandments,
even as I have kept my Father's commandments,
and live in his love.
All this I tell you
that my joy may be yours
and your joy may be complete.
This is my commandment:
love one another
as I have loved you."
(Jn 15:9-12)

I suspect the two were not always
as I found them that day
making their aged way along a lone path.
Then they were one
but I knew that such love did not come about
by wishing it so.

As I watched
it could be seen, without doubt,
that the man and the woman
had become for one another
living shillelaghs of strength and stability,
carved by one another,
and, over the years,
worn to stubby knobs
of twisted beauty,
polished and valued.

The Park Bench

His spirit
leaning on hers for life,
her frame
leaning on his for strength,
together, as one, they made their way
to a nearby bench,
slowly shuffling along the path
much as autumn shuffles into winter.
Their steps moved in perfect rhythm,
trustingly mated
as together,
now and one day,
they would slowly dance out of life
and into Life,
forever in love.

They had lived their love, I imagined and supposed,
through many deaths, but always into life,
through many hurts, but always into forgiving peace,
through so many divisions
that now there seemed only one love
unable to be divided further.
There were no more sides,
no more highs when the other was low,
no more rights when the other was wrong,
only one —
solely,
purely,
holy.

Two, who have grown one,
I have come to see,
hope in harmony
and speak with silence.
So it was, I thought, for them.
When she hurt, he wept;
and when he rejoiced, she smiled.

When she was ill, he grew weak;
and when he knew fear, she absorbed the darkness.

They had become one.

As they came upon the park bench
he noticed it dusty and soiled by the day.
Together, they made their way to a nearby tree.
Here he slowly moved out from under her leaning
and gently replaced himself with the tree.
She found strength there,
enough for him to return to the bench
and there, simply and briefly, brush it clean
with as much care as one would give
to a reigning throne.

Having prepared for the queen's approach
he made his way back to the tree.
She noted his care
and smiled
though there would have been no need,
Yet love is superfluous and generous beyond need.
He led her, then, to that park's lone bench,
and bent low as she leaned on him
so that he might ease her down gently.
Royalty must always appear graceful,
he seemed to muse,
and then he too smiled.
Having brought her to rest
he took his place beside her.
There they sat
as I watched from a distant grass.

In all the time that they presided
over the park and its surroundings
they never once spoke,

except, I suspect, with their hearts,
nor did their eyes ever meet,
though, perhaps it was, I thought,
because love sees more clearly.

I was about to take my leave
when I thought I saw her nod back ever so slightly.
A few moments passed
then again her head moved back
slowly
quietly
gently
and again
slowly
quietly
gently.

As she did so,
and just as slowly
he began to reach toward his side
and then behind his back.
Moments passed,
more and more unraveled,
her head and her breath nodded back
again
and
again.
Having reached behind him
and
just as slowly
he began to bring his arm around
from his back
now to the front
and across to her
and
as he held up to her his hand
and handkerchief —
she sneezed......

47

Slowly
the handkerchief was returned
and just as slowly
she smiled.
Thank you.
And the silence of her love echoed through my heart.

A gentle while passed
before they rose from the park bench
and made their way back, as they had come.
The man and the woman
spirits
lives
loves
one.

The Banjo Man

This story and the liturgy which surrounds it were originally created to prayerfully celebrate Independence Day, July 4. Following the usual introductory rites, the first scripture was proclaimed. A time of silent reflection followed. The story was then told, the climax and conclusion of which came in the song. Following the song, the Gospel was proclaimed, but without any introduction — almost as if it were part of the story itself. A prayer of the faithful, shaped around phrases from the Declaration of Independence, and a communion meditation are included here with these scriptures and story.

A reading from the letter of Paul to the Galatians (5:1, 13-25).

When Christ freed us, he meant us to remain free. Stand firm, therefore, and do not submit again to the yoke of slavery. My brothers, you were called, as you know, to liberty; but be careful, or this liberty will provide an opening for self-indulgence. Serve one another, rather, in works of love, since the whole of the Law is summarized in a single command: Love your neighbor as yourself. If you go snapping at each other and tearing each other to pieces, you had better watch or you will destroy the whole community.

Let me put it like this: if you are guided by the Spirit you will be in no danger of yielding to self-indulgence, since self-indulgence is the opposite of the Spirit, the Spirit is totally against such a thing, and it is precisely because the two are so opposed that you do not always carry out your good intentions. If you are led by the Spirit, no law can touch you. When self-indulgence is at work the results are obvious: fornication, gross indecency and sexual irresponsibility; idolatry and sorcery;

feuds and wrangling, jealousy, bad temper and quarrels, disagreements, factions, envy; drunkenness, orgies and similar things. I warn you now, as I warned you before: those who behave like this will not inherit the kingdom of God. What the Spirit brings is very different: love, joy, peace, patience, kindness, goodness, trustfulness, gentleness and self-control. There can be no law against things like that, of course. You cannot belong to Christ Jesus unless you crucify all self- indulgent passions and desires. Since the Spirit is our life, let us be directed by the Spirit.

This is the Word of the Lord.

A long, long time ago there was a tiny land called Freedom, no bigger than a whisper or a quiet smile of someone's gentle love. The people of Freedom had always lived freely, and in this they took great delight. They were free to come and go, to believe what they would, to share what they had. For all of these reasons the people of Freedom were happy. Often they would gather with one another — sometimes to tell stories, at other times to laugh and be silly, and yet at other times to be serious and discuss the weighty questions of life. It was on one such occasion that they found themselves asking one another, "Is the image of our founder on the front of the coin or on the back of the coin?" As always, there was disagreement. There were those who insisted that the image was on the front for it would be too demeaning to place it on the back. Others, of course, insisted it was on the back of the coin, holding that the nation's symbol — a sprouting seed — was of greater importance and should therefore be on the front of the coin. Finally someone suggested a vote. Whatever the outcome of the vote would be the solution to the question. This they did, and the problem was solved. Everyone in the land of Freedom was delighted at the simple solution to their dilemma, and they all began to sing and shout:

> Free to choose
> and have a common aim,
> life is easier
> when we're all the same.

It all seemed so simple, so efficient, so much better when everyone agreed. Thus they began to address new questions, always voting and always calling all to abide by the decision of the majority — for they were free, they said, and could choose as they wished. They voted on whether ice cream cones should have flat bottoms or pointed bottoms, deciding upon the flat so that people might be able to set them down and rest if they got weary. They voted on whether kites should fly with tails or without, deciding upon the tails so that they might issue licenses to fly them without. And they voted on whether shoes should be made with laces or with buckles, deciding upon laces lest children never learn how to tie knots. Always the majority decided for the minority, thinking it better if all were alike and proclaiming:

> Free to choose
> and have a common aim,
> life is easier
> when we're all the same.

After a time, decisions in the land of Freedom came to be arrived at without voting — simply by a sense of general agreement. It was decided that everyone should like sports, which made it difficult for those whose gifts and skills tended toward the arts. At another time it was decided that everyone should go to college, which made it difficult for those who particularly enjoyed working with their hands. On another occasion it was decided that everyone should marry, which made it difficult for those who had not fallen in love. Then too it was decided that everyone should live in a large home, which made it difficult for those who were already lonely and did not want more rooms. In time the people of Freedom decided that young was better than old and thin better than round and heavy. Always they made those decisions, saying:

> Free to choose
> and have a common aim,
> life is easier
> when we're all the same.

Because they no longer voted in the Land of Freedom, weighty decisions were made and imposed upon one another more frequently by a vague common agreement. It was decided that if one wished to pray, it had to be done in church, for people who prayed outside of church could not be real believers. It was decided, too, that the best way to fight for peace was through war, and those who chose to work for peace in other ways were imprisoned. It was also decided that no one should have more than two children, and that it was best if people who had reached a certain age no longer worked, for it seemed that by then they had outlived their usefulness.

Bit by bit the people of freedom were no longer free. There were many who were not of the majority and who were forced to live in ways they had not or would not have chosen. Always the others would insist:

> Free to choose
> and have a common aim,
> life is easier
> when we're all the same.

One day a stranger came to the land of Freedom. He noticed how many of its people were not free — free to have pointed ice cream cones or shoes with buckles. Perhaps, thought the stranger, if I become a teacher, I shall be able to teach them of these freedoms and open them to new and different ways of life. Unaware of the stranger's plans, the people hired him as a teacher. But within a month's time the people began to say to one another, "We mustn't have our children thinking this way, or soon we will no longer all be the same." So they came to him and told him he would no longer be free to teach their children.

The stranger thought, then, that he would call everyone to vote, as they had once done in years past. Perhaps then all would be allowed to be different. But the questions were not allowed on the ballot. So it was that, though the stranger had given much time and spent much effort, the people of Freedom became no freer.

Unable to share his dream, the stranger tucked a sack packed with clothes under one arm and a banjo packed with songs under the other, and left the village and tiny land of Freedom. Once he had crossed the border bridge, the stranger sat down under a tree, picked up his banjo, and unpacked the songs it held. He began to sing his simple songs of what should be — songs of peace and freedom, of forgiveness and freedom, of justice and freedom, of gentleness and freedom. As he sang, the children of Freedom heard the melodies and came running across the bridge. They delighted in the songs he sang, and soon they began to sing along. Indeed, the banjo man had captured their spirits.

As the children made their way home that night, the melodies lingered in their hearts, and their spirits sang joyfully. Once home, the children sang the songs to their parents, and together everyone delighted in the songs of the banjo man. As they sang the songs of peace and forgiveness, of justice and gentleness, little by little they grew to allow others to be different. Little by little the land began to be more free. They began to think that it was not important for everyone to be the same. They could be different and happy and free at the same time.

Year after year, season after season, they sang the songs of the banjo man. He would teach them new songs and sing again the old ones, and as long as they sang, they grew more and more free. In time, however, they began to wonder who would sing them songs of freedom and of what should be once the banjo man was no more, once he and his banjo would grow silent and fall asleep.

One day what they all had feared came to pass. The banjo man died. The people of freedom gathered to bury him, and when they did so, they thought it strange that his banjo could not be found. Nowhere was it to be seen. For days and weeks and months there were no more songs of what should be — no more songs of peace and freedom, of forgiveness and freedom, of justice and freedom, of gentleness and freedom. A year of silence unraveled and slowly the people of Freedom grew less free.

Then, one day, a song was heard once again in the land of Freedom, and the heavy silence floated away. The children shouted and laughed as they all came running. For so long they had been without a song that they had almost forgotten the joy and delight they once had known. Who was this banjo man, they wondered, who now came singing songs of freedom and of what should be — just as in days long passed. They listened closely, then, having gathered together, as the banjo man sang a story of freedom, a story of life and death and life again, a story of God's spirit in us all:

The Banjo Man

Words and Music by
BILL CALLAHAN

It's the ban-jo man__ and he un-der-stands__ what the
(3rd time) I un-der-stand

chil-dren all__ can see; and he sings them rhymes__ of

hap-py__ times__ in the land of "That should be." And the

chil-dren say that it's just that way, 'cause it's

all that they can see, and the ban-jo man__ is a

hap-py__ man__ 'cause he hopes e-ter-nal-ly.

Verse 1 And he told them of__ the good-ness__ in the

folks through-out__ the land, and how hearts beat the same, not af-

fec-ted by names or the col-or of the per-son's hands. And he

told them of the fu-ture, how they'd all grow up__ some

Angels To Wish By

day, but how dreams stay a - live, how they

will sur - vive — if you help them a - long the way. — It's the

Verse 2

Now the years were grand, — but they took the strength — of the

old man's wear-y hands, — and he won-dered what — the

chil-dren all — would do. — When his life had been com -

plet - ed, and his ban - jo was a - sleep, — would his

song of "That — should be" be end - ed, too? "Oh,

no, it shall be me," said John, of nine - teen years and one, and a

young man sought the ban - jo man's con-sent. "I won't

let you down, my friend; your song of "That should be" won't end. And the

old man hand-ed him — his in - stru - ment. — And the

56

young man sought out all the chil-dr-en___ and said,"I'm the

Yes, the ban-jo man___ is a hap-py___ man, and he

lives in you and me.

Jn 8:31-36

To the Jews who believed in him Jesus said:
    "If you make my word your home
    you will indeed by my disciples,
    you will learn the truth
    and the truth will make you free."
They answered, "We are descended from Abraham and we have never been the slaves of anyone; what do you mean, 'You will be made free?'"Jesus replied:
    "I tell you most solemnly,
    everyone who commits sin is a slave.
    Now the slave's place in the house is not assured,
    but the son's place is assured.
    So if the Son makes you free,
    you will be free indeed."
            This is the Gospel of the Lord.

THE PRAYER OF THE FAITHFUL

Lector:	"We hold these truths to be self-evident, that all men are created equal..."
All:	We pray, Father, that we, your people, may always share equally in your blessings. May those who are in want know the generosity

of those who have more. May your love in us know no bounds.

Lector: "We hold these truths to be self-evident..., that all men are endowed by their Creator with certain unalienable rights..."

All: When nations are oppressed by governments that deny human rights, we pray, Father, that your Spirit may move courageous people to stand up and call those governments to justice and peace.

Lector: "We hold these truths to be self-evident..., that among these rights are life, liberty and the pursuit of happiness..."

Men: Father, you are life. May all be fully alive.

Women: Lord Jesus, you died to free us from sin. May we grow in loving each other.

All: Spirit of God, you give us joy. May we be content with all that is simple.

Lector: "For the support of this..., with a firm reliance on the protection of Divine Providence, we mutually pledge to each other our lives, our fortunes and our sacred honor."

THE MEDITATION

Once, decades back, people bound themselves to one another for a common purpose — that being, to preserve the values they shared in common, values of peace and justice, of freedom and equality, of life and its holiness.

One by one other communities joined them — united in that common purpose.

1787	Delaware	1845	Florida
	Pennsylvania		Texas
	New Jersey	1846	Iowa
1788	Georgia	1848	Wisconsin
	Connecticut	1850	California
	Massachusetts	1858	Minnesota
	Maryland	1859	Oregan
	South Carolina	1861	Kansas
	New Hampshire	1863	West Virginia
	Virginia	1864	Nevada
	New York	1867	Nebraska
1789	North Carolina	1876	Colorado
1790	Rhode Island	1889	North Dakota
1791	Vermont		South Dakota
1792	Kentucky		Montana
1796	Tennessee		Washington
1803	Ohio	1890	Idaho
1812	Louisiana		Wyoming
1816	Indiana	1896	Utah
1817	Mississippi	1907	Oklahoma
1818	Illinois	1912	New Mexico
1819	Alabama		Arizona
1820	Maine	1959	Alaska
1821	Missouri		Hawaii
1836	Arkansas		
1837	Michigan		

Today, we who gather here do so because we share common values. We break bread and share a cup in the name of Jesus — pledging ourselves to him and to one another, believing that when we do so he is present with us — and with him, his peace and his justice, his life and his holiness.

Perhaps, Perhaps

When God had finished creating all that is and just before he breathed his spirit into it, he sat back and looked at everything he had made and saw that indeed it was good. God was pleased, not only with what he had created, but also with himself. "One thing remains," thought God, "that I give a home to what I have made." God then made a home for his creation, and he called that home Love. Thus when he breathed the spirit of life into all his creatures, they found themselves living in God, for God is Love. Then all that is was one with God, he living in them and they living in him. And God's people were happy.

As long as God's people lived in the home they had been given they were happy. Because they gathered in Love, they always knew warmth — never cold or loneliness. No one knew fear, and everyone felt safe and secure. There was no hunger, for the people were fed with God's Love. There was no illness, for Love could heal the deepest pain. There was no sadness, for the Love in which they lived offered them a joy and a peace more richly blessed than anything they could desire.

One day a stranger came into their land. He noticed immediately how everyone was happy and at peace and wondered why this was so. When he asked those he met, they always explained how they lived in Love, God's home for them. At first the stranger found great difficulty believing such an answer, but in time he heard that answer so often that he began to think, "Perhaps, perhaps."

One day the stranger asked those around him, "What will happen if God ever stops loving? Where, then, will you live?" "Oh, that is not possible," answered the people, "for God is Love and so God is always with us. We will always have a home." But the stranger only shrugged and said, "Perhaps, perhaps."

Time continued to unravel, and God's people continued to live in his Love. Yet the stranger could not help but wonder. "It is true," he said, "that God is Love and thus he will never cease loving you. But what will happen if you get lost and cannot find your way home. Then where will you live?" "Oh, that is not possible," answered the people, "for God is in all places. We cannot be lost, for wherever we are, God is there. And so we shall always have a home." But the stranger only shrugged and said, "Perhaps, perhaps."

Then one day the stranger told the people he would be leaving their land. He thanked them for their kindness and goodness, and said that before he left he had one more question. "It may be true that God is Love and thus he will never stop loving you," he said. "It may be true as well that God is in all places and thus you can never be lost. But what will happen if the day comes when people will no longer trust in one another to reveal

God's Love to them? Then where will you live?" As the stranger left their land, the people stood silent and then shrugged and said, "Perhaps, perhaps."

In the days that followed, the people began to ask the strangers' question to one another. "What would happen if in days to come people no longer loved? Then where would we live?" They grew frightened and fearful and hesitated to trust one another or those who would come after them.

One day soon thereafter, the elder in the land called all the people together. After all had arrived, he stood up in their midst. Though each one there knew well the story of the stranger who had come and asked question, the elder told the story once more. "Though each of us believes that God is Love and that he will always Love us, though each of us believes that God is present in all that is and that we can never be lost, perhaps we should take steps to preserve that Love should those who come after us cease to remember that we ourselves must reveal it." The people all nodded, and then shrugged their shoulders in helpless agreement, "Perhaps, perhaps."

"What shall we do?" they asked the elder. "How can we preserve the Love that is home for us? Tell us, if you know." The elder was not sure, but he thought he had a plan. "If we take portions of our home, of the Love in which we live, if we shape that Love into bricks and bake them in our ovens, if we preserve our Love in such a way, then should the day ever come when those who follow us cease to reveal God's Love, there shall yet be Love in what we have preserved."

"No, no!" shouted a young girl. "That cannot be, for then the Love in which we live will be cold and harsh. Then Love will have died, for Love must be warm and gentle." And the people all shrugged and said, "Perhaps, perhaps." An old man then stood up and walked to the center of the people. He looked at them in silence and finally spoke. "The young girl is right, for if we try to preserve our Love as you suggest, it will grow old and weak. Love must renewed each day. Only in that way can it remain strong." But the people only shrugged and said, "Perhaps, perhaps."

Then the elder stood up once more. "What the young girl and the old man say may be true, but then again it may not, for we have never lived outside of our home. Indeed it is because we love that we try to preserve the home in which we live. We must trust in the work of our hands. We must not be led astray by our hearts." And the people only shrugged and said, "Perhaps, perhaps."

That night the young girl wept, and the old man shed many tears of sadness. They felt like strangers in a foreign land without a home.

In the days that followed, all who were able worked to preserve the Love in which they lived. They carved out portions of their home and shaped them into bricks. They baked those bricks in their ovens until they grew hard and rigid. Later, after

the baked portions of their home had grown cold, they piled the bricks high — monuments to a time past.

Before long, though no one took notice except the young girl and the old man, a change slowly took place. Occasionally someone would grow hungry or weak from illness. Others were left alone, weary from the labor and no longer able to be of use. One or two even seemed to disappear and were seen no more, though a few thought that perhaps they had gotten lost and could not find their way home.

One day the elder gathered all who lived in the land. "What we once feared would occur has taken place," he explained. "The home of love in which we once lived has all but disappeared. Many are lonely and cold. Others grow hungry and ill. The God who was Love is no more. We are a people without a home. Fortunate and wise were we to prepare for a day such as this. Look about you, my people, and see the Love we have preserved. We must go to a new land. We shall take with us the work of our hands and build for ourselves a new home — strong and high. There we shall live and know God once more in the work of hands. Does it not seem best that we follow such a plan?" And the people who had gathered only shrugged and said, "Perhaps, perhaps."

A reading from the book of Genesis

Throughout the earth men spoke the same language, with the same vocabulary. Now as they moved eastwards they found a plain in the land of Shinar where they settled. They said to one another, "Come, let us make bricks and bake them on the fire." For stone they used bricks, and for mortar they used bitumen. "Come," they said "let us build ourselves a town and a tower with its top reaching heaven. Let us make a name for ourselves, so that we may not be scattered about the whole earth."

Now Yahweh came down to see the town and the tower that the sons of man had built. "So they are all a single people with a single language!" said Yahweh. "This is but the start of their undertakings! There will be nothing too hard for them to do. Come, let us go down and confuse their language on the spot so that they can no longer understand one another." Yahweh scattered them thence over the whole face of the earth, and they stopped building the town. It was named Babel therefore, because there Yahweh confused the language of the whole earth. It was from there that Yahweh scattered them over the whole face of the earth. (Gen 11:1-9)

This is the word of the Lord.

The people, having built their tower, made it their temple. There they came to pray. There they came to find their God. This they did until the time of Jesus. It was Jesus who taught us how to build a new temple — a temple of living stones — a home once more made of a Love that is warm and gentle and filled with kindness.

A reading from the first letter of Paul to the Corinthians.

You are God's building. Thanks to the favor God showed me, I laid a foundation as a wise master-builder might do, and now someone else is building upon it. Everyone, however, must be careful how he builds. No one can lay a foundation other than the one that has been laid, namely Jesus Christ.

Are you not aware that you are the temple of God, and that the Spirit of God dwells in you? If anyone destroys God's temple, God will destroy him. For the temple of God is holy, and you are that temple. (1 Cor 3:9-11, 16-17)

This is the word of the Lord.

Advent is a time given to the task of building that new temple of living stones. Advent is a time given to the discovery that Jesus reveals God's Love in us in the way we are good to one another. In this way Jesus continues to be born through us.

A SUGGESTED ACTIVITY

What follows now is an explanation of an Advent activity for the students. A large poster "Temple" has been prepared before hand, looking something like this:

Behind each brick is the name of one or more of the children in the class(es). One of the bricks is removed each school day of Advent to reveal the name of someone in the class. The one whose name is revealed thus becomes a living stone, part of that new temple. That person is to be treated specially that day in school (no homework, special privileged work, extra kindness shown, whatever). The next day that person removes another brick to reveal a new living stone. Teachers' names should be included. The number of bricks should be accurately calculated to correspond to the number of school days in the Advent Season. The cornerstone is revealed last and is, of course, the Lord Jesus. It is best if the children are not told who the cornerstone will be, and thus they discover at the end of the Advent Season who is most important in their lives.

The concluding message of Advent is that by our kindnesses we have become the place where people gather to find the presence of God. We are the new home of God, the temple made of living stones. The following scripture might be used for the final day.

A reading from the letter of Paul to the Ephesians

You are strangers and aliens no longer. No, you are fellow citizens of the saints and members of the household of God. You form a building which rises on the foundation of the apostles and prophets, with Christ Jesus himself as the main cornerstone. Through him the whole building is fitted together and takes shape as a holy temple in the Lord; in him you are being built into this temple, to become a dwelling place for God in the Spirit. (Eph 2:19-22)

This is the word of the Lord.

givingthanksgiving

This Thanksgiving Day prayer is a paraliturgy probably best suited for small groups of children, though the story itself can certainly be used as part of a parish Thanksgiving Eucharist, particularly one at which families are in attendance. Beginning with a joyful song of thanks or praise, a song that is spirited and fun to sing, sets the tone for the entire celebration. A prayer recognizing God's generosity and goodness follows. The Word of God is then proclaimed.

A reading from the book of Deuteronomy

Moses told the people: "The Lord, your God, is bringing you into a good country, a land with streams of water, with springs and fountains flowing in hills and in valleys, a land of wheat and barley, of vine and fig trees and fruit trees, of olive trees and of honey, a land where you can eat bread without end and where there is nothing you will need, a land whose stones contain iron and in whose hills you can mine copper. When then you finish eating all you wish, when then you are filled, you must bless the Lord, your God, for all that he has given you. (Deut 8:7-10)

The following story is told best with the children seated on the floor and gathered about the storyteller. In addition to God, there are three characters in this story: Sun, Day, and Autumn. Three

68

large cue cards are needed for telling the story, one
for each of the three characters. The cue card for
Sun contains the words "Burn, Burn, Burn;" for
Day, "Yeaaaaaa;" and for Autumn, "Ahhhhhh."
Throughout the story, whenever the characters are
mentioned (as indicated by ***), the storyteller
taps the child holding the corresponding card. The
child then raises the card high over his head, and
the congregation reads it aloud. A bit of
impromptu practice before the story actually
begins will set the mood of fun and participation.
The story follows:

It was the time for beginning, and God had just completed
the season of summer. Before long, summer traveled on into
autumn. During these days all of God's creation took great
delight in the things they could do. Why there was Sun *** who
warmed all that was. And there were long Days *** when people could play and celebrate their friendship. And then, of
course, there was Autumn *** with all of her beautiful colors.
Yet soon a strange thing happened. As Autumn began to move
into December, all of God's creatures seemed to lose their gifts.
Sun *** began to grow cold and did not warm as he once did.
Long Days ***, once filled with good times and play, began to
lose their light and grow shorter and shorter and shorter. Why
even Autumn *** lost all of her color and became gray and
dreary and dark. Thus they all began to weep, because to them it
seemed they had lost all they had once been given. The three
then decided to do what they could to regain their blessings.
    Though fearful, Sun *** and Autumn *** and Day *** all
made their way to God. "God, we would like to talk to you."
"What seems to be the matter?" asked God. "We're losing
everything we've been given," was their reply. Sun *** was the
first to speak up: "Everything is turning cold." Just as quickly
Day *** spoke up as well: "I'm losing all my light." And finally

Autumn *** rose up: "I lost all my color." God heard them and then explained. "Oh, you don't understand. Why Sun, it is true you lost all of your warmth. But now people huddle inside to keep warm. I'm giving to you all of these people who huddle together and find each other's love." Then Autumn *** interrupted: "But what about me? I lost all of my beauty." "Oh," said God in reply, "to you I'm giving people who now, rather than sit around and look how beautiful *you* are, gather together to keep warm and see the beauty in *each other*. Thus I'm giving you people who appreciate each other's love." Finally Day *** stood up and asked, "What about me?" God simply sighed. "That's just what I've been talking about. Don't you see? When I give you more darkness, I am giving you people who choose to be inside to share their blessings. So you see, Sun and Autumn

and Day, you should not be crying because of all you lost; you should be happy because of all that I have given you." Having said that, God began to return to his heavens. But when he saw all of them crying once more he said, "Now what's the matter? I've just explained how much I've given you." It was Autumn ***, then, who stood up and explained, "We're not crying because of how much we lost. We're crying out of joy because of how much you've given us."

And so it is that at the time of Thanksgiving we are called upon to look at our blessings and to forget all that we have lost. You see, all year long we are tempted to think of those times when we might have lost God's love by our sinfulness. Thanksgiving comes to say "No — look at all of those times when you discovered God's love in his forgiveness." All year long we are tempted to be sad because of a friend we have lost or because someone we love has died. But at the time of Thanksgiving we are called to look around us and see all of the other friends we have and all of the people who love us. All year long we are tempted to feel sad because someone took our wallet or tore our coat; we see blessings that other people have and we do not. But at Thanksgiving we are asked to look at all of the other marvelous gifts we do have. So it is that we come together, professing faith in the Lord Jesus, and finding a tear in our eyes, not because we are sad over all that we have lost, but because we are filled with joy over how much we have been given.

A reading from the holy Gospel according to

Jesus said to his disciples:
"I tell you truly:
you will weep and mourn
while the world rejoices;
you will grieve for a time,
but your grief will be turned into joy.
You are sad for a time,

but I shall see you again;
then your hearts will rejoice
with a joy no one can take from you." (Jn 16:20 & 22)

At this time attention should focus upon the bread. As the prayer leader stands before the bread or holds it in his or her hands, he or she invites the children to explore the number of different ways people say thank you. (Examples will include saying thank you with words, a smile, a hug or kiss, a handshake, and a gift.) He or she then explains that those who believe in Jesus say thank you to God by giving and sharing bread with one another. That is the Christian way of giving thanks. The prayer leader then explains that at this prayer the group will give thanks to God by sharing bread — but that they should do so in silence. In addition, no one may ask for bread, but must wait in silence until it is offered to them. Finally, it is best if everyone waits to eat until each person has received a portion of the bread. The prayer leader then takes the bread in his or her hands and uses one or a combination of the following blessing forms:

1. A blessing prayer of his or her own — simple, brief, to the point.

2. A time of silent prayer when all ask God to bless the bread about to be shared.

3. A simple sign of the cross over the bread by the prayer leader.

Those present pray the Our Father, and then share the bread in silence. A reminder that all share the bread in silence and that all wait until it is offered might be helpful. Once all of the children have given thanks by sharing the bread, a simple song of thanks and praise can be a suitable closing.

Lucy Light

The story of Lucy and the light she brings is a gem of folklore treasure. Her name means *light,* and consequently she became patron of many who looked for new light. She became patron of the eyes, the lights of the body, patron of lamplighters, who brought light to dark neighborhoods, and patron of Venitian gondoliers, who paddled the canals and sang "Santa Lucia."

Historically, Lucy was one of the three great "girl saints" — Barbara, Catherine, and Lucy — who were beheaded in Sicily during the persecution of Diocletian. Her feast became set on December 13, which, until the reform of the calendar, was the shortest day of the year.

Apparently there was a strong appeal to Lucy and her light among the Scandinavian countries, where winters could be particularly long and dark. In Norway and Sweden, much folklore and custom centered upon Lucy and her light. On December 12, the eve of her feast, children would write *lussi* and draw figures of her on doors and gates and walls. The *lussi* and drawings were intended to break the spell of winter darkness and to announce to the evil spirits that the usn with its light would now begin its return. Lucy-fires burned throughout the land and people threw in incense with the hope that the smoke might touch them and protect them from dangers, disease and evil spirits. As the fires burned, trumpets and flutes announced the end of growing darkness and the return of the sun and new light.

Each year the youngest girl in a family or village would be invited to be Lucy for the feast. Bearing cakes, cookies and candies, and dressed in a long, white gown with a wreath of burning candles in her hair, she would awaken people from their sleep and announce the gift of Lucy-light — how old mister sun had been awakened to begin a new course of new light for a darkened world. The story at the core of that tradition now follows.

Those who dwelled in the cold, winter lands of the North lived by the sun, sleeping with the nighttime and rising with the first light of the day. So it was that as the Season of Autumn journeyed toward the Season of Winter, the people of the North went to bed earlier and earlier, and rose later and later, for it was during this time of year that the nights grew longer and longer and the days shorter and shorter. In this land of winter snows it only snowed during the nighttime, and so the people of the North never saw it snow, for they always went to bed as the sun set, and always rose with the sun and the new day.

It happened on one of those long, dark nights that young Lucy and her family went to bed as usual with the setting sun. However, on this particular occasion, Lucy awoke much earlier than usual. She awoke while it was yet dark and before the sun had given birth to another day. No longer sleepy, Lucy quietly slipped down the stairs and went to the family kitchen. There she made candies and cookies for her family — all sorts of sweets and delights. The cookies she placed in the oven, and while she waited for them to bake, she opened the heavy, wooden door leading to the fields and forests behind her home. Surprised and amazed, Lucy stood in the doorway, filled with delight at seeing what she had never seen before — large, crystal snowflakes gently finding their way to trees and fence posts, to roof tops and roadways.

Karen Dewey

Lucy grew so excited over her new discovery that she began to dance and to sing. She sang songs of joy and happiness and praise — all the while spinning and dancing out in the yard. As she did so, the snowflakes continued to fall, gently nesting in her hair, flickering like candlelight against the nighttime sky. In her excitement, Lucy danced faster and faster and sang louder and louder — so much so that old mister sun awoke a little bit earlier that morning to see who it was that was causing all he disturbance.

Once the sun had begun to rise and awake the day, the snow no longer fell, and Lucy, thrilled and excited, returned inside her home. There she gathered her cookies and candies to serve her family as they came down for the new day. They had become her morning prayer.

Lucy was so taken up by the beauty of the winter snows that during the next night she awoke a little bit earlier, again prepared candies and cookies for her family, and while they baked, she again went outdoors to sing and dance amid the falling snow. Again the singing and dancing awoke old mister sun, only on this morning a little bit earlier than on the morning before. Each day thereafter Lucy always awoke a little bit earlier than the morning before, and each day thereafter old mister sun would also begin a new day a bit earlier as well, rising to see who it was that was causing the disturbance.

Now you, too, know why it is that from this day the days begin to grow longer and longer and the nighttimes shorter and shorter.

While the story is delightful all by itself, it comes at a most appropriate time of year when we celebrate the advent of the true light of the world, the Lord Jesus. The following is suggested as a possible prayer service or Liturgy of the Word, perhaps for December 13, the feast of St. Lucy, or perhaps for December 21, the shortest day of the year. It would seem that the spirit of the season would allow either.

The following materials are needed for the prayer: one or two large candles, lit throughout the prayer; individual candle tapers, such as those used for the Easter Vigil Service, of sufficient number to provide at least one for each person; a candle holder for the tapers — either a large bowl filled with sand, or a box painted or covered with foil, with sufficient holes in the cover to hold all of the candles when lit; a box of Christmas cookies and candies, wrapped as a Christmas gift.

A comfortable and informal setting is appropriate for the prayer, perhaps a carpeted area, particularly if this is with a small group of children. It is helpful if the room can be darkened. The large candles are lit, and the candle holder and tapers lying next to it should be centrally located. The wrapped cookies should be visible, but set to one side.

The prayer begins with a song that picks up the theme of light. Scripture follows:

**What we have seen and heard
we are telling you
so that you too may be in union with us,
as we are in union
with the Father
and with his Son Jesus Christ.
We are writing this to you to make our own joy complete.
This is what we have heard from him,
and the message that we are announcing to you:
God is light; there is no darkness in him at all.
If we say that we are in union with God
while we are living in darkness,
we are lying because we are not living the truth.
But if we live our lives in the light,
as he is in the light,
we are in union with one another.
1 Jn 1:3-7a**

Our prayer is a verbal expression of what we work for, of what our lives are about. Thus our prayer and our actions are light, and we become one with God who is light. Having briefly explained this, and with the lights off or dimmed, invite those present to light a taper, place it in the holder, and share their prayer — their way of being light.

After all who wish have offered a prayer, tell the story of Lucy, a story of a girl who brought back the sun, who brought light to other people. A second sharing of scripture follows:

Jesus said:
"I am the light of the world;
anyone who follows me will not be walking in the dark;
he will have the light of life."
Jn 8:12

If the above is a Liturgy of the Word, then the Liturgy of the Eucharist follows immediately. If the above is a prayer service, conclude with a common prayer or the Our Father. At the conclusion of the Eucharist or prayer service, open the wrapped Christmas cookies and share Lucy's gifts with all present.

The Seal

The Judeo-Christian scriptures are a story: the tale of a people's journey into faith. Whenever the believing community gathers, portions of that story are told and retold lest the story be forgotten. Indeed, we are a story-people.

What follows here is a story. In its entirety it is meant to be the Liturgy of the Word for the Feast of All Saints, November 1. The scriptures for that feast (Rv 7:2-4, 9-14; Mt 5:1-12; 1 Jn 3:1-3) are woven into the telling of the story and do not occupy a place in the liturgy apart from the telling of the story.

Sixteen large banners are necessary for telling the story: eight ghosts and eight saints, which are hung back-to-back, saints against ghosts, on banner stands or poles. The banners should be large, at least five feet high and two and a half feet wide. The banners can be made out of paper for ease of construction. The ghosts might be made of colored paper for the sake of visual variety, though white paper would be suitable as well. Make the saints out of white paper with colored neck-pieces and draw their faces with a magic marker.

The ghosts are shaped as in figure 1; eyes and names are in contrasting colored paper. Each ghost has a name: MACHO MAN, MR. COOL, MEAN MACHINE, NUMERO UNO, MADAM GUILLOTINE, SOMORE, HAWK, OUCHLESS. The saints are the same size and shape as the ghosts, which allows them to be placed back-to-back on the poles.

Two readers are necessary, one a lector and one an off-stage voice of God who reads the beatitudes over a microphone. Nine junior high students were originally used in the story — eight were banner carriers and the ninth was an angel dressed in a white, hooded acolyte's robe. The banners were positioned in the sanctuary area, ghost-face down, before the liturgy began. They were arranged throughout the sanctuary in a random, scattered pattern, and appeared alternately from each side of the sanctuary.

The lines proclaimed by the angel and the saints (banner holders) are memorized. Whoever is able to project with the greatest volume should be chosen as the angel, since the angel has the only line spoken aloud individually and without a microphone.

The children, without the banners, process in with the celebrant and take their places, seated on the floor near their banners. The angel is positioned in the center of the sanctuary. After the story is told the children take their places in the pews. They return to the sanctuary area after communion and carry the banners (saints' faces toward the congregation) as part of the recessional.

I first met Michael in a green, wooded, daydream portion of Milwaukee called Hawthorne Glen. How it was that I met him is a story for another time. What should be known at this time, however, is that Michael is very small, indeed no more than ten inches tall: twelve at the most. He himself insists that he is an angel, and, while he does not look like what you or I might expect an angel to look like, it may very well be that Michael is just that, an angel.

A short time ago I went to Hawthorne Glen, hoping that I might again come upon my friend, Michael, and indeed I did.

The glen itself, as I have said, is wooded, with slow paths that drift in and out of the greenery, which is everywhere. At one end of the glen is a large field often used by the children of the area for baseball and soccer.

On this particular morning, I was the only one in the glen. It happened to be a warm, sunny, autumn day, and so I lay on my back in the middle of the field, feeling the warmth of the sun as it showered the field. For a moment I closed my eyes, and in that instant I suddenly felt a weight on my chest. Just as quickly I sat up, only to realize that in doing so I knocked Michael off my chest and onto the ground. There he was, grumbling and complaining that I had knocked him down and didn't I know any better. I apologized quickly, as he brushed himself off, knowing that he would be eager to get on with the visit.

"Michael," I began, "may I ask you a question? Would you mind?"

"Oh, I know," said Michael. "You're wondering why there's so much evil in the world, and you would really like some sort of explanation of it all."

"You're right, Michael. That's what I was wondering, but I never told anybody else," I said in surprise. "How did you know my question?"

"Because I'm an angel," he replied. "Don't you remember? I told you that before. Angels always know what other people are wondering."

And then I remembered. I had learned that lesson many times before. Always I had forgotten. "Well? Aren't you going to tell me?" I asked. I could hardly wait, for Michael always had such good explanations.

"It all comes down to the ghosts," answered Michael.

At this point, all eight banners are raised, revealing the eight ghosts.

"The ghosts?" I said, wondering aloud. "Are you sure?"

"Yes, yes," he insisted. "It's the ghosts. Haven't you heard the story?" I had to confess I had not, and so Michael went on to tell the story.

"A long, long time ago, shortly after the beginning of creation, there was a violent, cosmic battle over who would rule all that is. There were those who won and those who lost, of course. Those who won wanted God to rule. That was us," said Michael, obviously quite proud. "And those who lost, well, they came to be known as devils.

"Shortly thereafter, because they were angry that they had lost and because they still wanted to rule, the devils sent ghosts out over the land: ghosts who would win over all the goodness. This all began to take place during the month of October. As the days grew shorter and shorter and colder and colder, as the nights grew longer and longer and darker and darker, the ghosts were carried by the wind out over the land and among the people. As soon as the people began to realize what was taking place, they rushed indoors. They grew frightened and fearful and huddled inside their own homes. No longer did they dare to go out or visit other homes. Before long, they began to stop loving and forgiving as they once did — all because they began to forget they were friends of one another. It was a sad time, indeed, for God and for us angels.

"God began to ask around for suggestions, hoping to find a solution. I must confess, it was my idea," said Michael, again quite proud, "and God did think it was a good idea."

"Oh, that's great, Michael," I told him. "What did you do? How did you solve the problem? You've got to tell me."

"Oh, I didn't do it," answered Michael. "God did it. It was just my idea. But it was a good idea. I'm sure glad I came up with it."

"Well, what did God do?" I wanted to know the answer, and I was beginning to grow quite excited.

"God decided to take one day of goodness and slip it in very quietly between the end of October and the beginning of November. God called that day All Saints Day. He figured if he could slip a day of goodness into the middle of all those ghosts, into the middle of all that darkness, why, then no one would forget to be good and to be holy."

"Did it work? How did he do it? What happened?" I wanted to know in the worst way.

"It's in the book," said Michael. "The story is in the book. Look in the book."

"What book?" I asked. "Where is it?"

"Don't you remember? I gave you a book a long time ago with all the stories in it. Look in that book."

I turned to look around me, hoping to find the book, and when I turned back to ask Michael where it was, Michael was gone.

At this point, all eight ghost banners are lowered.

He had disappeared, as quickly as he had come. But there, not far from where I sat, I saw the book that Michael had once given me, long before. I opened the book, and this is what I found:

At this point, the celebrant hands the lectionary to the lector to begin reading. As the lector begins the reading, the angel rises slowly to his feet and extends his arms outward so that his whole person forms a cross.

Lector: "I, John, saw another angel come up from the east holding the seal of the living God. He cried out at the top of his voice to the four angels who were given power to ravage the land and the sea."

Angel: "Do no harm to the land or the sea or the trees until we imprint this seal of the foreheads of the servants of our God."

Lector: **"I heard the number of those who were so marked; one hundred and forty-four thousand from every tribe of Israel."**

It was then that God's angel went from ghost to ghost, there to plant the seal of the living God on each.

As each ghost is introduced, the banner depicting that ghost is lifted up. The angel then goes before that banner and bows low at the waist, remaining bowed until the description is completed. This is done for each ghost.

The angel of the Lord came before the ghost Macho Man. "Never allow anyone to know you are weak or in need. Never show that you are poor — poor in strength, poor in health, poor in wisdom, poor in wealth. Always be strong. Never be poor. Always be macho." Thus spoke the ghost Macho Man. Then the angel of the Lord sealed that spirit +.

In each instance, at this point, the angel stands up straight and traces with his hands a huge cross over the ghost, from top to bottom and side to side. This having been completed, the banner is turned to reveal the saint on the opposite side.

And the voice of God was heard to say, **"Blest Are The Poor In Spirit, The Reign Of God Is Theirs."**

Spoken by an offstage voice.

Then the angel came before the ghost Mr. Cool. "Never cry or show emotion or people will get to you. Never be sensitive or easily swayed. Never be overly involved. Always be cool." Thus spoke the ghost Mr. Cool. Then the angel of the Lord sealed that spirit +, and the voice of God was heard to say, **"Blest Are Those Who Mourn, They Shall Be Comforted."**

Then the angel came before the ghost Mean Machine. "Take care lest you be kind and people take advantage of you. Be competitive. Be a winner. Be on top at all costs. Be aggressive." Thus spoke the ghost Mean Machine. Then the angel of the Lord sealed that spirit +, and the voice of God was heard to say, **"Blest Are The Gentle, They Shall Inherit The Earth."**

Then the angel came before the ghost Numero Uno. "Always be number one, regardless of who might get hurt. Thirst for self, always, and only for self, and you shall be satisfied. If you do not care for yourself, who will?" Thus spoke the ghost Numero Uno. Then the angel of the Lord sealed that spirit +, and the voice of God was heard to say, **"Blest Are Those Who Hunger And Thirst For What Is Right, They Shall Be Satisfied."**

Then the angel came before the ghost Madam Guillotine. "Never give anyone a second chance. Hold people to their deeds, for if you forgive, they shall repeat their deeds. Stand firm." Thus spoke the ghost Madam Guillotine. Then the angel of the Lord sealed that spirit +, and the voice of God was heard to say, **"Blest Are The Merciful, They Shall Have Mercy Shown To Them."**

Then the angel made his way before the ghost Somore. "You shall want all that is. You shall desire all things: video recorders and 10-speed bikes, IZOD clothes and Cadillacs and somore and somore and somore and somore..." Thus spoke the ghost Somore. Then the angel of the Lord sealed that spirit +, and the voice of God was heard to say, **"Blest Are The Single-Hearted, For They Shall See God."**

Now the angel of the Lord made his way before the ghost Hawk. "You must believe in the power of might, the power of fear that controls. You must believe that might makes right, that might makes peace, and be ready to fight for it. You must believe that war can bring peace." Thus spoke the ghost Hawk. Then the angel of the Lord sealed that spirit +, and the voice of God was heard to say, **"Blest Are The Peacemakers, They Shall Be Called Children Of God."**

Finally the angel stood before the ghost Ouchless. "Seek life without pain. Seek life without suffering. It is your heritage. You have a right to it: a right to life without pain." Thus spoke the ghost Ouchless. Then the angel of the Lord sealed that spirit +, and the voice of God was heard to say, **"Blest Are They Who Suffer In The Cause Of What Is Right, The Reign Of God Is Theirs."**

> At this point, all the banners should be up, facing the people and showing the face of a saint.

And the story then continued in the book Michael had once given to me.

Lector: **"After this I saw before me a huge crowd which no one could count from every nation, race, people, and tongue. They stood before the throne and the Lamb, dressed in long white robes and holding palm branches in their hands. They cried in a loud voice,**

Saints: **'Salvation is from our God, who is seated on the throne, and from the Lamb!'**

Lector: **"All the angels who were standing around the throne and the elders and the four living creatures fell down before the throne to worship God."**

> At this time, all eight banners lean forward slightly, as if to bow. The angel, standing in the center, lifts his arms to the heavens as if in a gesture of prayer and praise.

"Amen! Praise and glory, wisdom, thanksgiving, and honor, power and might to our God forever and ever. Amen!"

> The banners are again brought straight up, and the angel lowers his arms to his sides and again bows his head.

"Then one of the elders asked me, 'Who do you think these are, all dressed in white? And where have they come from?' I said to him, 'Sir, you should know better than I.' He then told me, 'These are the ones who have survived the great period of trial; they have washed their robes and made them white in the blood of the Lamb.'"

So it is that Michael's story was about to come to an end. I realized then that we who gather are the saints, those who are called to live values which differ so often from society's values. We who are the believers are called to overcome the evil present about us. We who have been sealed are called to be the sign of God's goodness. Finally, one last time I returned to the book Michael had given me, and this is what I found:

At this time, all the banner bearers stand and hold the saints high while the reading is proclaimed.

Lector:

A reading from the first letter of John.

"See what love the Father has bestowed on us in letting us be called children of God! Yet that in fact is what we are. The reason the world does not recognize us is that it never recognized the Son. Dearly beloved, we are God's children now; what we shall later be has not yet come to light. We know that when it comes to light we shall be like him, for we shall see him as he is. Everyone who has this hope based on him keeps himself pure, as he is pure."
This is the Word of the Lord.

The Story

In recent times storytelling has regained a recognized place in American tradition. For the person of Christian faith, however, *the* story will always be that of the Lord Jesus — *his* birth, *his* comings and goings, *his* stories, and ultimately the story of *his* death and resurrection. Whenever believers gather, they find themselves telling and retelling his story. It is in the remembering of the story that faith is shared and that faith remains strong.

Unfortunately, one's strength is often one's weakness as well, and so it is with the frequent telling of the Jesus story. Too often the Gospel story is so familiar that when it is told, it loses its staying power. We say, "Oh, I've heard this one before," and the Gospel rerun syndrome allows us to switch mental channels.

It was out of this concern that the following form for Luke's passion narrative was created to be used in the Palm Sunday Eucharist celebration. The congregation simply listened and watched. There were no parts for "All." The passion narrative was proclaimed by three voices: the narrator, Jesus, and the speaker. Additional voices could have been used to distinguish the various roles. Background to the proclamation varied, including silence, organ, strings, and flute.

The passion narrative was divided into scenes, each projected on a screen by an overhead projector. The film was a continuous sheet of paper, the width of the overhead projector glass. Geometric shapes, representing the individuals in the passion narrative, were cut out of the paper and covered with colored transparencies to give the different shapes their different colors.

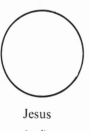

Jesus
(red)

Apostles
(blue)

Judas
(purple)

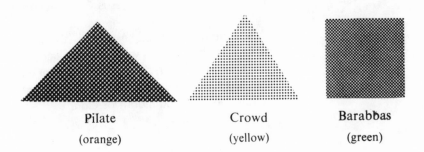

Pilate
(orange)

Crowd
(yellow)

Barabbas
(green)

The purpose of this style of proclamation was to draw the hearers into the message of the Gospel more deeply. It was an effort to make a familiar story new in its impact. We hoped it would remain forceful and powerful, yet gentle and quiet.

Narrator: The Passion of our Lord Jesus Christ according to
                Luke.
                When the hour arrived, Jesus took his place at the
                table, and the apostles with him. He said to them:
Jesus: "I have greatly desired to eat this Passover with you
                before I suffer. I tell you, I will not eat again until it
                is fulfilled in the kingdom of God."

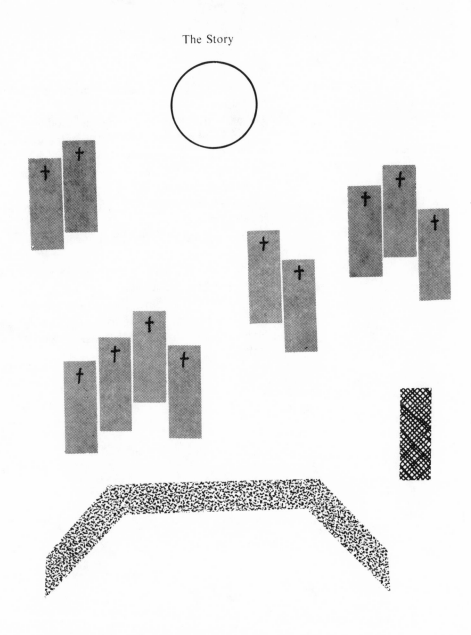

Narrator:	Then taking a cup he offered a blessing in thanks and said:
Jesus:	"Take this and divide it among you; I tell you, from now on I will not drink of the fruit of the vine until the coming of the reign of God."
Narrator:	Then, taking bread and giving thanks, he broke it and gave it to them, saying:
Jesus:	"This is my body to be given for you. Do this as a remembrance of me."
Narrator:	He did the same with the cup after eating, saying as he did so:
Jesus:	"This cup is the new convenant in my blood, which will be shed for you!
	"And yet the hand of my betrayer is with me at this table. The Son of Man is following out his appointed course, but woe to that man by whom he is betrayed."

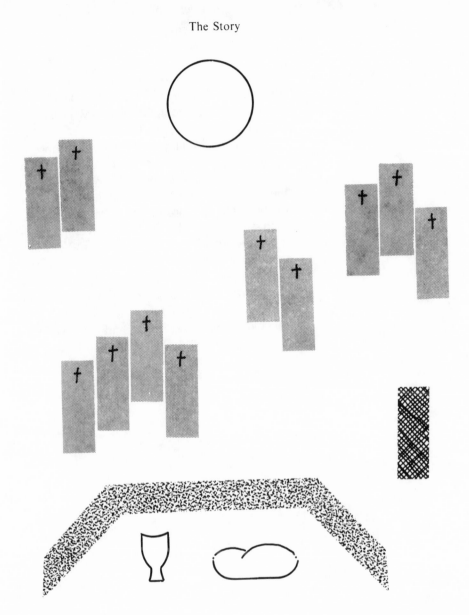

Narrator: Then they began to dispute among themselves as to which of them would do such a deed.

A dispute arose among them about who should be regarded as the greatest. He said:

Jesus: "Earthly kings lord it over their people. Those who exercise authority over them are called their benefactors. Yet it cannot be that way with you. Let the greater among you be as the junior, the leader as the servant. Who, in fact, is the greater — he who reclines at table or he who serves the meal? Is it not the one who reclines at table? Yet I am in your midst as the one who serves you. You are the ones who have stood loyally by me in my temptations. I for my part assign to you the dominion my Father has assigned to me. In my kingdom you will eat and drink at my table, and you will sit on thrones judging the twelve tribes of Israel.

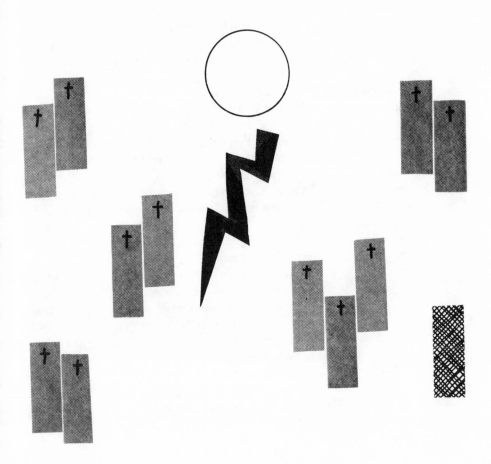

	"Simon, Simon! Remember that Satan has asked for you to sift you all like wheat. But I have prayed for you that your faith may never fail. You in turn must strengthen your brothers."
Narrator:	Peter said to him,
Speaker:	"Lord, at your side I am prepared to face imprisonment and death itself."
Jesus:	"I tell you, Peter, the cock will not crow today until you have three times denied that you know me."
Narrator:	And then he asked them all,
Jesus:	"When I sent you on mission without purse or traveling bag or sandals, were you in need of anything?"
Speaker:	"Not a thing."
Narrator:	He said to them:
Jesus:	"Now, however, the man who has a purse must carry it; the same with the traveling bag. And the man without a sword must sell his coat and buy one. It is written in Scripture, 'He was counted among the wicked,' and this, I tell you, must come to be fulfilled in me. All that has to do with me approaches its climax."
Speaker:	"Lord, here are two swords!"
Jesus:	"Enough."

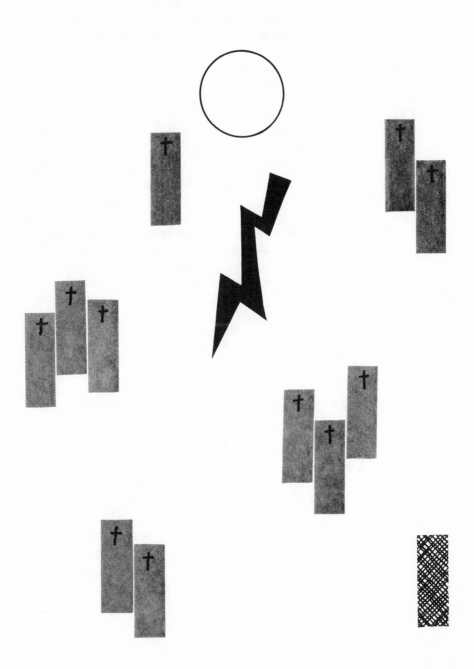

Narrator: Then he went out and made his way, as was his custom, to the Mount of Olives; his disciples accompanied him. On reaching the place he said to them,

Jesus: "Pray that you may not be put to the test."

Narrator: He withdrew from them about a stone's throw, then went down on his knees and prayed in these words:

Jesus: "Father, if it is your will, take this cup from me; yet not my will but yours be done."

Narrator: An angel then appeared to him from heaven to strengthen him. In his anguish he prayed with all the greater intensity, and his sweat became like drops of blood falling to the ground. Then he rose from prayer and came to his disciples, only to find them asleep, exhausted with grief. He said to them,

Jesus: "Why are you sleeping? Wake up, and pray that you may not be subjected to the trial."

Narrator: While he was still speaking a crowd came, led by the man named Judas, one of the Twelve. He approached Jesus to embrace him. Jesus said to him,

Jesus: "Judas, would you betray the Son of Man with a kiss?"

Narrator: When the companions of Jesus saw what was going to happen, they said,

Speaker: "Lord, shall we use the sword?"

Narrator: One of them went so far as to strike the high priest's servant and cut off his right ear. Jesus said in answer to their question,

Jesus: "Enough!"

Narrator: Then he touched the ear and healed the man. But to those who had come out against him — the chief priests, the chiefs of the temple guard, and the ancients — Jesus said,

Jesus: "Am I a criminal that you come out after me armed with swords and clubs? When I was with you day after day in the temple you never raised a hand against me. But this is your hour — the triumph of darkness!"

Narrator: They led him away under arrest and brought him to the house of the high priest, while Peter followed at a distance. Later they lighted a fire in the middle of the courtyard and were sitting beside it, and Peter sat among them. A servant girl saw him sitting in the light of the fire. She gazed at him intently, then said,

Speaker: "This man was with him."

Narrator: He denied the fact, saying,

Speaker: "Woman, I do not know him."

Narrator: A little while later someone else saw him and said,

Speaker: "You are one of them too."

Narrator: But Peter said,

Speaker: "No, sir, not I!"

Narrator: About an hour after that another spoke more insistently:

Speaker: "This man was certainly with him, for he is a Galilean."

Narrator: Peter responded,

Speaker: "My friend, I do not know what you are talking about."

Narrator: At the very moment he was saying this, a cock crowed. The Lord turned around and looked at Peter, and Peter remembered the word that the Lord had spoken to him, "Before the cock crows today you will deny me three times." He went out and wept bitterly.

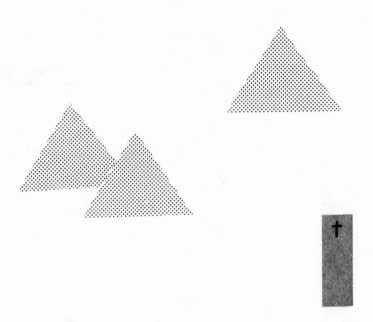

Meanwhile the men guarding Jesus amused themselves at his expense. They blindfolded him, and then taunted him:

Speaker: "Play the prophet; which one struck you?"

Narrator: And they directed many other insulting words at him.

At daybreak, the elders of the people, the chief priests, and the scribes assembled again. Once they had brought him before their council, they said,

Speaker: "Tell us, are you the Messiah?"

Narrator: He replied,

Jesus: "If I tell you, you will not believe me, and if I question you, you will not answer. This much only will I say: 'From now on, the Son of Man will have his seat at the right hand of the Power of God.' "

Narrator: They asked in chorus,

Speaker: "So you are the Son of God?"

Narrator: He answered,

Jesus: "It is you who say I am."

Narrator: They said,

Speaker: "What need have we of witnesses? We have heard it from his own mouth."

Narrator: Then the entire assembly rose up and led Jesus before Pilate. They started his prosecution by saying,

Speaker: "We found this man subverting our nation, opposing the payment of taxes to Caesar, and calling himself the Messiah, a king."

Narrator: Pilate asked him,

Speaker: "Are you the king of the Jews?"

Narrator: He answered,

Jesus: "That is your term."

Narrator: Pilate reported to the chief priests and the crowds,

Speaker: "I do not find a case against this man."

Narrator: But they insisted,

Speaker: "He stirs up the people by his teaching throughout the whole of Judea, from Galilee, where he began, to this very place."

Narrator: On hearing this pilate asked if the man was a Galilean; and when he learned that he was under Herod's jurisdiction, he sent him to Herod, who also happened to be in Jerusalem at the time. Herod was extremely pleased to see Jesus. From the reports about him he had wanted for a long time to see him, and he was hoping to see him work some miracle. He questioned Jesus at considerable length, but Jesus made no answer. The chief priests and scribes were at hand to accuse him vehemently. Herod and his guards then treated him with contempt and insult, after which they put a magnificent robe on him and sent him back to Pilate. Herod and Pilate, who had previously been set against each other, became friends from that day.

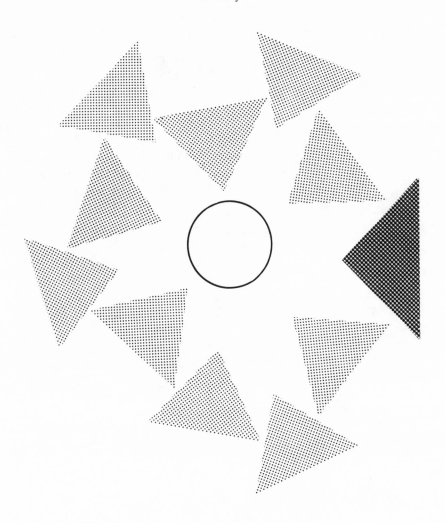

Speaker:

Pilate then called together the chief priests, the ruling class, and the people, and said to them:
"You have brought this man before me as one who subverts the people. I have examined him in your presence and have no charge against him arising from your allegations. Neither has Herod, who therefore has sent him back to us; obviously this man has done nothing that calls for death. Therefore I mean to release him, once I have taught him a lesson."

Narrator:	The whole crowd cried out,
Speaker:	"Away with this man; release Barabbas for us!"
Narrator:	This Barabbas had been thrown in prison for causing an uprising in the city, and for murder. Pilate addressed them again, for he wanted Jesus to be the one he released. But they shouted back,
Speaker:	"Crucify him, crucify him!"
Narrator:	He said to them for the third time,
Speaker:	"What wrong is this man guilty of? I have not discovered anything about him that calls for the death penalty. I will therefore chastise him and release him."
Narrator:	But they demanded with loud cries that he be crucified, and their shouts increased in violence. Pilate then decreed that what they demanded should be done. He released the one they asked for, who had been thrown in prison for insurrection and murder, and delivered Jesus up to their wishes.
	As they led him away, they laid hold of one Simon the Cyrenean who was coming in from the fields. They put a crossbeam on Simon's shoulder for him to carry along behind Jesus. A great crowd of people followed him, including women who beat their breasts and lamented over him. Jesus turned to them and said:
Jesus:	"Daughters of Jerusalem, do not weep for me. Weep for yourselves and for your children. The days are coming when they will say, 'Happy are the sterile, the wombs that never bore and the breasts that never nursed.' Then they will begin saying to the mountains, 'Fall on us,' and to the hills, 'Cover us.' If they do these things in the green wood, what will happen in the dry?"

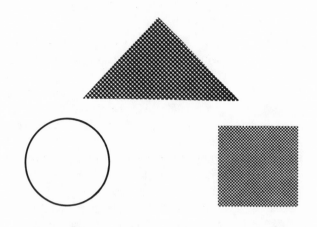

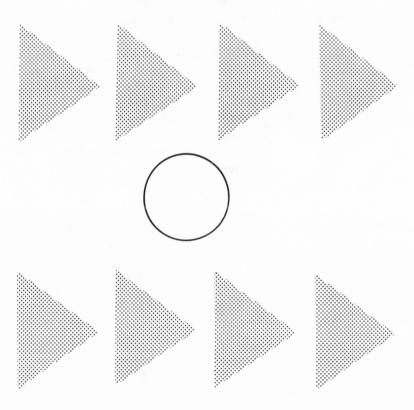

Narrator: Two others who were criminals were led along with him to be crucified. When they came to Skull Place, as it was called, they crucified him there and the criminals as well, one on his right and the other on his left. Jesus said,

Jesus: "Father, forgive them; they do not know what they are doing."

Narrator: They divided his garments, rolling dice for them. The people stood there watching, and the leaders kept jeering at him, saying,

Speaker: "He saved others; let him save himself if he is the Messiah of God, the chosen one."

Narrator: The soldiers also made fun of him, coming forward to offer him their sour wine and saying,

Speaker: "If you are the king of the Jews, save yourself."

Narrator: There was an inscription over his head: "This is the King of the Jews." One of the criminals hanging in crucifixion blaphemed him:

Speaker: "Aren't you the Messiah? Then save yourself and us."

Narrator: But the other one rebuked him:

Speaker: "Have you no fear of God, seeing you are under the same sentence? We deserve it, after all. We are only paying the price for what we've done, but this man has done nothing wrong. Jesus, remember me when you enter upon your reign."

Jesus: "I assure you: This day you will be with me in paradise."

Narrator: It was now around midday, and darkness came over the whole land until midafternoon with an eclipse of the sun. The curtain in the sanctuary was torn in two. Jesus uttered a loud cry and said,

Jesus: "Father, into your hands I commend my spirit."

Narrator: After he said this, he expired.

(Pause)

The centurion, upon seeing what had happened, gave glory to God, by saying,

Speaker: "Surely this was an innocent man."

Narrator: When the crowd which had assembled for this spectacle saw what had happened, they went home beating their breasts. All of his friends and the women who had accompanied him from Galilee were standing at a distance watching everything.

There was a man named Joseph, an upright and holy member of the Sanhedrin, who had not been associated with their plan or their action. He was from Arimathea, a Jewish town, and he looked expectantly for the reign of God. This man approached Pilate with a request for Jesus' body. He took it down, wrapped it in fine linen, and laid it in a tomb hewn out of the rock, in which no one had yet been buried.

That was the Day of Preparation, and the sabbath was about to begin. The women who had come with him from Galilee followed along behind. They saw the tomb and how his body was buried. Then they went home to prepare spices and perfumes. They observed the sabbath as a day of rest, in accordance with the law.

Why Water Lost Her Color

No more than a breath had passed after God had finished his creating when Water began to complain to God. "Hey! Hey, you up there!" shouted Water. "Are you God or aren't you? I've got a complaint."

While God was not too pleased with being called "Hey, you ," he was also patient and decided upon another day for teaching manners to his new creation. "Yes," he confessed, "I am God, and if you've got a complaint, you've come to the right person. You're obviously not very happy with my creation plan. What seems to be the problem?"

"The problem," replied Water, "is my color. I'm dark and murky and dreary. No one thinks I'm very attractive. None of the animals will come and drink at my shore. The birds won't fly overhead because they can't see anything swimming around; and the fish are all dying because I'm so muddy. I really think you better do something about this, and, if I do say so myself, you'd better do it soon — with all due respect."

"Well," asked God, "What color would you like to be? Any preferences?"

"No. I don't care. As long as I'm not so muddy and dirty and dark. You're God — you work it out. But please do hurry."

"Tomorrow," answered God. "Tomorrow's enough time. Today I'm tired and I'm going to rest. Tomorrow will be soon enough."

Early the next morning God slipped down from his heaven-home before any of his creation had discovered that the sun was his alarm clock. He quietly slipped up to Water's edge while she was still sleeping. For a few moments he watched her — still, quiet, not even a ripple, silently asleep.

"GOOD MORNING!!!!" shouted God. With that loud greeting, Water was so startled that her waves began to pound the shore, fighting against what she thought for a moment was an attacker. Her waves grew high and thundered and roared and splashed and sprayed, but only for a moment, as she quickly realized it was God who had startled her so.

"Well," remarked Water, "you certainly do make a grand entrance. I'm glad to see you're a God who's prompt and keeps promises. Now, how you gonna fix me up?"

God said nothing. He simply smiled and began to breathe his breath out over Water. He began to breathe his spirit into Water, and as he did so, Water grew clearer and clearer, until soon she had no color at all, except the color of the sun that brought light and warmth and life. Within that moment, animals began to come to drink, and birds flew overhead playing tag with the waves, and fish danced on their tails over the face of Water who was happy to share in the new life.

Indeed, it was a time for celebrating. Water was most pleased and forever grateful to the God who had made her; and God was able to go back to his heaven-home and delight again in his creation. So now you, too, know the story of why water is crystal clear.

Together this story and the ritual are intended to be a time of prayer. Singing is a valuable addition and, when it is incorporated into the prayer, enhances the prayer a great deal. This story/prayer has been used both with adults and with children, even as young as first grade, and always it has been prayerful.

The ritual necessitates a large bowl, preferably transparent, of punch bowl size, and partially filled with water, as well as a large glass pitcher of water. No scripture has been suggested here, though something appropriate could certainly be incorporated — perhaps before telling the story. Those who gather should be seated in a circle (a carpeted area works best) with the bowl and pitcher of water in the center.

Upon completing the story, the leader invites all to share a prayer focusing upon the gift of life, for water is a symbol of that gift. It is helpful to relax everyone if it is explained that it is not necessary for everyone to offer a prayer. Those who wish to share a prayer first pour a small amount of water from the pitcher into the bowl, and then offer their prayer. In a random sort of way those who wish to pray come to the center, one-by-one, and do so.

After all who have wished to share a prayer have done so, the leader explains that the bowl now contains, in effect, our prayers. Yet perhaps there are still unspoken prayers which need to be added somehow. Thus the leader holds the bowl in his hands and invites everyone to breathe out over the water, for our breath is the Spirit of God, the breath of God in us. As we breathe out over the water, we breathe into the water all of our hopes and dreams and prayers for life. Together, then, with the leader, all breathe over the water, and as they do so the leader gently rocks the water, as if to suggest the Spirit of God entering the water.

The leader then explains that he or she will move among them with the bowl of water, the bowl which now holds their prayers for life. As the leader does so, all are invited to place their hands deep into the water and then sign themselves with the water, thereby showing their acceptance of and participation in the prayers of one another. It is valuable to explain, as well, that when one touches the water, one should do so without fear of getting wet — to reach deep, to feel the water, to allow it to touch him or her. Too often we seem to be so gentle with water, lest we get wet. It does not stain. It cannot harm us. We need to become friends with God's gift of life.

Having completed the above ritual, a common praying of the Our Father or a suitable song provides a prayerful conclusion. Amen.

The Bag Lady

This storyprayer has 4 major portions — scripture, story, meditation, and response. Each part flows into the next with minimal comment. As with all communal prayer, a gathering song at the beginning is valuable toward creating a sense of oneness. A song at the conclusion might also be considered.

The Word of God is proclaimed with the aid of an overhead projector as described earlier in this collection (cf. "The Story", page 89). This gospel narrative consists of six scenes. The use of soft background music contributes to creating a reflective mood and helps to highlight the gospel story in contrast to the contemporary story which follows.

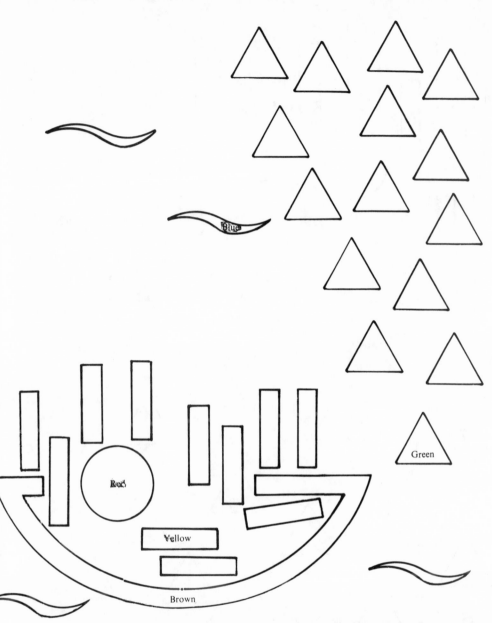

The apostles returned to Jesus and reported to him all that they had done and what they had taught. He said to them, "Come by yourselves to an out-of-the-way place and rest a little." People were coming and going in great numbers, making it impossible for them to so much as eat. So Jesus and the apostles went off in the boat by themselves to a deserted place. People saw them leaving, and many got to know about it.

Mk 6:30-33a

Angels To Wish By

People from all the towns hastened on foot to the place, arriving ahead of them. Upon disembarking Jesus saw a vast crowd. He pitied them, for they were like sheep without a shepherd; and he began to teach them at great length.

Mk 6:33b-34

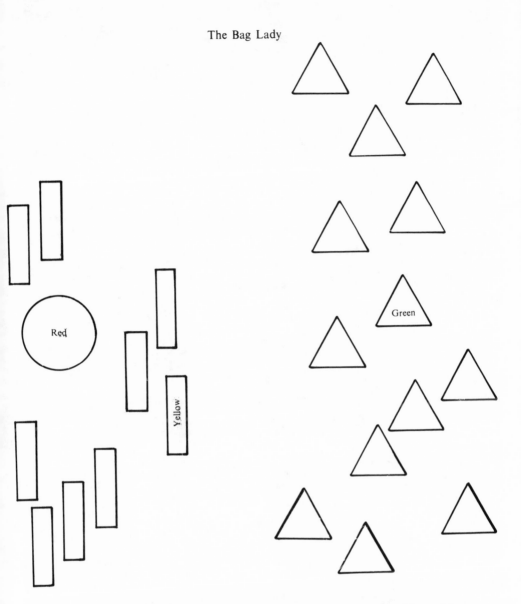

It was now getting late and his disciples came to him with a suggestion: "This is a deserted place and it is already late. Why do you not dismiss them so that they can go to the crossroads and villages around here and buy themselves something to eat?" "You give them something to eat," Jesus replied. At that they said, "Are we to go and spend two hundred days' wages for bread to feed them?" "How many loaves have you?" Jesus asked. "Go and see."

Mk 6:35-38a

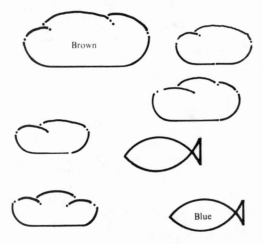

Brown

Blue

When they learned the number they answered, "Five, and two fish."

Mk 6:38b

He told them to make the people sit down on the green grass in groups or parties. The people took their places in hundreds and fifties, neatly arranged like flower beds. Then, taking the five loaves and the two fish, Jesus raised his eyes to heaven, pronounced a blessing, broke the loaves, and gave them to the disciples to distribute. He divided the two fish among all of them and they ate until they had their fill.

Mk 6:39-42

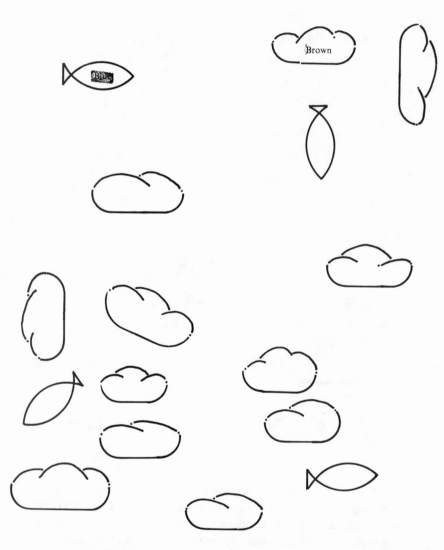

They gathered up enough leftovers to fill twelve baskets, besides what remained of the fish. Those who had eaten the loaves numbered five thousand men.

Mk 6:43-44

THE STORY

Doorbells and presents are always filled with surprises, perhaps because they both come wrapped in the unexpected. And when the doorbell is the occasion for a gift, the delight in our spirits often multiplies to such intensity that once again we thrill at the child within. This is one such story. However, I caution you that though it is a story about children, it will ask you to transform your innocence into courage.

The doorbell rang, and when I opened the door I found an older lady, who looked very much like one of the bag-ladies of State Street in Milwaukee. They carry all that they own in shopping bags, and, for the most part, support themselves by asking for quarters and nickels and dimes from passers-by. That person who came to my door was very much like such a bag-lady. She said to me, "Could I please talk to you?" In the back of my mind I thought I knew what it was she wanted to talk about — a quarter or a dollar or what she then needed. Nevertheless, I said, "Sure!" and invited her in to be seated.

"I would like to give you something," she began. "In fact there are two things I would like to give you." I thought such a comment to be rather inside-out, for usually the bag-ladies come asking, yet this one came offering. "I would like to give you a story," she continued, "but it is a very different kind of story, for it goes back a long way. It happened before you were born. It happened before I was born, before our mothers and fathers were born. It happened a long, long time ago — I don't even remember the years anymore.

"In a land far, far away, there was a tucked-away village. In the center of that village was a small table, and on that table there was always a loaf of bread. Yet no one ever ate of the bread; no one ever took the bread. For, you see, there were all kinds of stories which roamed about the village — stories of people who had taken the bread and had become slaves. Thus, no one took the bread for fear of becoming a slave. Other stories told of people who had taken the bread and had disappeared. Thus, no one

129

took the bread for fear of being seen no more. Still other stories were told of people who had taken the bread and had died. Thus, no one ever took the bread for fear that he too would die. No one ever remembered who it was who had taken the bread and had become a slave or had disappeared or had died. But people did remember the stories, and that was all that mattered.

"There was a ritual in this village that whenever a young boy or a young girl turned fourteen he or she would be brought to the table in the center of the village. There the elder of the village would stand opposite the youth with the table between them, and all of the other villagers would gather around. The elder would then ask the young boy or the young girl, 'Do you wish to take the bread?' Always out of fear of becoming a slave or of disappearing or of dying, the young boy or the young girl would say, 'No.' Three times the elder would ask the young person simply to make sure the question was clearly understood. All three times the young person would answer, 'No'."

As the bag-lady went on, I thought to myself how strange this story was. But long before I had discovered that when stories come from places you do not expect, they often bear truth within them.

The bag-lady went on. "One day a young boy turned fourteen and was brought froth to the table in the center of the village. As prescribed by the ritual the elder stood opposite the young boy, and all of the people of the village gathered around. The elder looked at the young boy and asked, 'Do you wish to take the bread?' This time the young boy said, 'Yes.' In surprise the people all gasped, for no one had ever said yes. Then the elder inquired once more, 'Do you wish to take the bread?' Again the boy replied, 'Yes.' One more time, having explained all of the different stories about slavery and disappearance and death, the elder asked, 'Do you wish to take the bread?' For the third time the boy said, 'Yes.' At that, everyone in the village stepped back. The boy walked forward and took the bread in his hands.

"What happened in the days that followed," said the bag-lady, "is that the boy didn't become a slave. What did happen is that he began to go about doing all kinds of good for people,

good that no one else would ever do for any one. You might say
that he became more of a servant, for anything that anyone
would ask he would do. And he did disappear for a while. Not
forever, but it seems that as the stories came back to the village,
he was among the people telling them about a God who loved
them so deeply that no matter what they would do, he would
still love them. Then one day he did return. And you ask, 'Did he
die?' Well, because the boy would do anything for anyone, and
because he went about telling them about a God who loved
them, and because it disturbed the people so much that they
could not be what he invited them to be, one day they did kill
him. Yet the word soon spread among the people that he still
lived among them."

Then, suddenly, the bag-lady got up from her chair and
walked out the door. I began to follow her, but she left quickly.
As I came back inside bewildered, I noticed that she had left her
bag. Carrying the sack, I ran out the door and to the street, but
there was no one there. I looked up and down the street, unable
to understand how someone could disappear so quickly. Then,
holding her bag, I walked back inside thinking about her story
and about the boy who once took the bread. Not knowing what
was in her bag and without even looking, I reached in to see
what it was she had left. Suddenly I was frightened, for I found
bread in the bag, and realized then that I too had taken the
bread. I began to wonder if I would become a slave, if I would
disappear to be seen no more, or if I too would soon die. In the
end it crossed my mind that perhaps this was the bag-lady's
second gift. I could not help but wonder if perhaps she and that
young boy of fourteen were the same person.

Before you leave today, someone will come to you and offer
you bread. Then you too will have to decide whether or not you
will take the bread. In that moment remember the story of the
bag-lady and remember, too, how we are asked to die each day
for one another. Above all else, however, when someone comes
and offers you bread, consider for a moment what life would be
if no one ever took the bread. Then, having considered such a
possibility — decide and choose.

THE MEDITATION

Two possible ways of incorporating the song, "Listen to the Bread," with accompanying action are suggested here for use as a meditation to follow the story. Both incorporate bread to be shared during the response.

The first possibility is simply to arrange to have "Listen to the Bread" sung following the story while someone else slowly and ceremoniously carries bread forth to the center. As that person reaches the front, he or she turns to face those gathered. With head bowed, he or she stands in silence, holding the bread while the song is concluded.

The second possibility necessitates a large brown paper bag, obviously wrinkled and well worn (as perhaps the bag lady may have carried). The bag contains a loaf of bread and is placed on the floor near where the story will be told. As the story is told and during the second last paragraph, the storyteller incorporates the bag into the telling of the story. At the appropriate time ("Not knowing what was in her bag and without even looking, I reached in to see what it was she had left."), the bread is lifted out of the bag. The story is concluded as the storyteller holds the bread. He or she continues to hold the bread, standing silently and with head bowed, as "Listen to the Bread" is sung.

Listen to the Bread

Words by
JOSEPH J. JUKNIALIS

Music by
SUSAN A. SAJDAK

Let the eyes of your spi-rit lis-ten to the bread speak.

Let the eyes of your spi-rit lis-ten to the bread.

(Last time only)

Lis-ten to the bread now gent-ly call your name.

1. It will whis-per a new dawn; it cries out to the noon-day sun.

1. Lis-ten to the bread now gent-ly call your name.

2. Break and share this gift. Je-sus is your life. Pain and
3. The lonli-ness you've known is shattered with a kiss. Peace was

2. suf-f'ring of-fered death is raised to life.
3. once for-got-ten. Our spirits now are healed.

D. C.

Lis-ten to the bread now gent-ly call your name.

No one ever remembered who it was who had taken the bread and had become a slave or had disappeared or had died. But people did remember the stories, and that was all that mattered.

"There was a ritual in this village that whenever a young boy or a young girl turned fourteen he or she would be brought to the table in the center of the village. There the elder of the village would stand opposite the youth with the table between them, and all of the other villagers would gather around. The elder would then ask the young boy or the young girl, 'Do you wish to take the bread?' Always out of fear of becoming a slave or of disappearing or of dying, the young boy or the young girl would say, 'No.' Three times the elder would ask the young person simply to make sure the question was clearly understood. All three times the young person would answer, 'No'."

As the bag-lady went on, I thought to myself how strange this story was. But long before I had discovered that when stories come from places you do not expect, they often bear truth within them.

The bag-lady went on. "One day a young boy turned fourteen and was brought froth to the table in the center of the village. As prescribed by the ritual the elder stood opposite the young boy, and all of the people of the village gathered around. The elder looked at the young boy and asked, 'Do you wish to take the bread?' This time the young boy said, 'Yes.' In surprise the people all gasped, for no one had ever said yes. Then the elder inquired once more, 'Do you wish to take the bread?' Again the boy replied, 'Yes.' One more time, having explained all of the different stories about slavery and disappearance and death, the elder asked, 'Do you wish to take the bread?' For the third time the boy said, 'Yes.' At that, everyone in the village stepped back. The boy walked forward and took the bread in his hands.

"What happened in the days that followed," said the bag-lady, "is that the boy didn't become a slave. What did happen is that he began to go about doing all kinds of good for people, good that no one else would ever do for any one. You might say that he became more of a servant, for anything that anyone would ask he would do. And he did disappear for a while. Not forever, but it seems that as the stories came back to the village, he was among the people telling them about a God who loved them so deeply that no matter what they would do, he would still love them. Then one day he did return. And you ask, 'Did he die?' Well, because the boy would do anything for anyone, and because he went about telling them about a God who loved them, and because it disturbed the people so much that they could not be what he invited them to be, one day they did kill him. Yet the word soon spread among the people that he still lived among them."

Then, suddenly, the bag-lady got up from her chair and walked out the door. I began to follow her, but she left quickly. As I came back inside bewildered, I noticed that she had left her bag. Carrying the sack, I ran out the door and to the street, but there was no one there. I looked up and down the street, unable to understand how someone could disappear so quickly. Then, holding her bag, I walked back inside thinking about her story and about the boy who once took the bread. Not knowing what was in her bag and without even looking, I reached in to see what it was she had left. Suddenly I was frightened, for I found bread in the bag, and realized then that I too had taken the bread. I began to wonder if I would become a slave, if I would disappear to be seen no more, or if I too would soon die. In the end it crossed my mind that perhaps this was the bag-lady's second gift. I could not help but wonder if perhaps she and that young boy of fourteen were the same person.

Before you leave today, someone will come to you and offer you bread. Then you too will have to decide whether or not you will take the bread. In that moment remember the story of the bag-lady and remember, too, how we are asked to die each day for one another. Above all else, however, when someone comes and offers you bread, consider for a moment what life would be if no one ever took the bread. Then, having considered such a possibility — decide and choose.

THE STORYTELLER'S LIBRARY

Storytelling Resources

Balloons! Candy! Toys!, *by Daryl Olsziewski, $8.95*
Story as a Way to God, *by H. Maxwell Butcher, $11.95*
Storytelling Step by Step, *by Marsh Cassady, $9.95*
Telling Stories Like Jesus Did, *by Christelle Estrada, $8.95*

Other Story Collections

The Stick Stories, *by Margie Brown, $7.95*
Parables for Little People, *by Larry Castagnola, $7.95*
More Parables for Little People, *by Larry Castagnola, $7.95*
A People Set Apart, *by Jean Gietzen, $6.95*
The Magic Stone — and Other Stories for the Faith Journey,
by James Henderschedt, $7.95
The Topsy Turvy Kingdom, *by James Henderschedt, $7.95*
Biblical Blues: Growing Through Setups and Letdowns,
by Andre Papineau, $7.95
Breakthrough: Stories of Conversion, *by Andre Papineau, $7.95*
Jesus on the Mend: Healing Stories, *by Andre Papineau, $7.95*
For Give: Stories of Reconciliation, *by Lou Ruoff, $7.95*
No Kidding God, Where Are You?, *by Lou Ruoff, $7.95*

Ask for these titles at your local library or bookseller, or write to:

 Resource Publications, Inc.
160 E. Virginia Street, Suite #290
San Jose, CA 95112-5848